With a surge of strength, Lara leaped from the top of the tree trunk, flipping toward the dais. A flicker took shape at the top of the silvery-blue liquid column, then became the Triangle piece.

Powell reached for the piece, but Lara snapped a hand out and grabbed it only inches from the man's fingers. The silvery-blue column collapsed, splashing across the dais and running into rivulets carved into the tomb's floor.

Lara landed in a crouch on the other side of the dais from Powell. With her free hand, she drew one of her .45s and trained it on the man. In the next heartbeat, the weapons of the security team lit her up with laser sights.

"Miss Croft," Powell said pleasantly. "It seems I underestimated you."

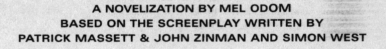

LARA CROFT TOMB RAIDER

A NOVELIZATION BY MEL ODOM
BASED ON THE SCREENPLAY WRITTEN BY
PATRICK MASSETT & JOHN ZINMAN AND SIMON WEST

A MINSTREL® BOOK

Published by POCKET BOOKS

New York   London   Toronto   Sydney   Singapore

This book is a work of fiction. Names, characters, places and incidents are products of the author's imagination or are used fictitiously. Any resemblance to actual events or locales or persons, living or dead, is entirely coincidental.

A MINSTREL PAPERBACK *Original*

 A Minstrel Book published by
POCKET BOOKS, a division of Simon & Schuster, Inc.
1230 Avenue of the Americas, New York, NY 10020

ISBN: 0-7434-2301-1

First Minstrel Books printing June 2001

10 9 8 7 6 5 4 3 2 1

A MINSTREL BOOK and colophon are registered trademarks of Simon & Schuster, Inc.

Interior book design by Jaime Putorti

Printed in the U.S.A.

PROLOGUE

Venice, Italy

The ornate building towered above Venice's famed Grand Canal. The sun dappled the old stone with gold, and rime showed along the foundation at the Canal's edge. It was one of the premiere spots in the city.

Atop the building, a gargoyle held a strange symbol in one long-taloned claw. The symbol was a triangle that held the etched relief of the All-Seeing Eye. The Eye was the standard of the Illuminati, the secret true power behind many governments and business interests.

In the biggest room on the top floor of the building, men and women, all of them fabulously wealthy and world renowned for their successes, sat around a conference table. They were the Illuminati.

Attorney Manfred Powell sat with them, calm and apparently unaffected by the air of tension in the room.

His law clerk, Pimms, sat just behind Powell. Pimms was several years younger than Powell and nowhere near as cool as his employer.

A distinguished gentleman, who appeared to be the Illuminati leader, addressed the group. "Brothers and sisters, it seems we are running out of time. This is not acceptable, Mr. Powell. The explanation for this, please?"

Pimms swallowed hard.

Powell spoke. "I have no *explanation*, and certainly no excuses, except to once again respectfully remind the Council that we are working from clues based on ancient cosmological models."

The High Council leader said nothing.

Powel continued speaking rapidly. "Clues predating Ptolemy, predating Aristotle, before Plato, models of the universe derived from hypotheses never recorded in the pages of history. That correlation between these models and the actual universe as we now know it has proved somewhat of a code-breaking challenge. But I am happy to announce that we are almost ready. And I am supremely confident that we will have our answer in time for the relevant planetary alignment."

"In one week."

"Yes."

"That's good news then, Mr. Powell," said the distinguished gentleman, "because, remember, we have only one opportunity to find what we are looking for. And if we fail, we must wait another five thousand years. So we *will* be ready?"

Powell answered the challenge calmly, "Trust me."

❖   ❖   ❖

After the meeting of the High Council had adjourned, everyone left but Pimms and Powell. Powell opened his notebook computer and began reviewing endless lines of code.

Pimms turned to Powell and asked anxiously, "You told the High Council leader that we were ready. But we're not ready, are we?"

Powell looked him squarely in the eye. "No."

"Oh my God. *My God!* We need a miracle."

"Shut up, Pimms! Stop whining!" Powell hissed. "Start praying."

ONE

Croft Manor, England

Lara Croft hung upside down by a rope attached to the high ceiling beam. The floor was wreathed in shadows far below.

Nothing moved in the darkness shrouding the room.

The world's greatest adventurer slid down another couple of inches along the rope. She knew she wasn't alone in the room. Her body straight and perfectly parallel to the rope, she made her decision between heartbeats, and turned loose.

Lara dropped through the darkness, twisting her body like a cat, and landed in a crouch. Her eyes raked the darkness as dust puffed at her feet.

A line of stone idols and massive statues loomed in the darkness around her.

Her sixth sense, developed from years of facing countless dangers in hundreds of hostile situations across the globe, tripped, snapping her into motion. She launched herself into an all-out run between the statues. Her dark braid slapped at her back with every long stride.

She was clad for battle, dressed in black shorts and sleeveless shirt. Fingerless gloves offered some protection to her hands, and her feet were encased in steel-toed combat boots. Twin pistols rode in quick-release holsters at her hips.

Sudden movement behind a statue directly ahead drew Lara's immediate attention. A long metal arm shot out of the shadows, a flashing blade at the end of the inhuman appendage.

Lara dodged to the left, heading toward another stone totem. Before she got behind it, a huge spiked fist shattered the totem's head into thousands of pieces.

Lara drew her .45s as she raced around the statues. A series of turns brought her to the heart of the maze. She turned again, then spotted the shimmering disk suspended in the shaft of light ahead.

The huge droid dropped between Lara and the shimmering disk. It stood nearly seven feet tall, a huge mass of steel and cybernetic tech. Six arms jutted out from the barrel-shaped trunk, each ending in a scythe-like blade capable of cutting her in half.

Lara slid through the dust. She dropped and skidded across the floor on her back. She brought the .45s up and fired as she slid toward the huge droid.

The droid leaned down, its metallic body gleaming as it focused on her.

Uh oh, she thought.

The droid drew back an arm—which now ended in a spiked fist—and struck. She moved quickly, but the force of the punch sunk the spikes deeply into the floor, trapping the droid's arm. The droid punched with another spiked fist, driving it deeply into the floor.

Lara wriggled but couldn't free herself from between the arms. The droid held up an arm. The scythe at the end of the arm disappeared into the forearm housing and a drill reappeared in its place.

The drill screamed to life. Mercilessly, the droid leaned down, shoving the drill at Lara's unprotected face. It was so close, she could read its directive on its sensor: KILL LARA CROFT.

"Oh, I don't think so," Lara stated defiantly. She planted both steel-toed boots between the droid's legs with a loud clang.

The droid kept the drill coming.

Lara pushed against the droid. The droid rose, and toppled, falling up and over Lara, thudding against the floor.

Freed, Lara vaulted to her feet. She scooped the pistols from the floor and turned to face the droid.

The droid detached the two arms spiked to the floor. It retracted all its remaining hands and brought out spiked claw fists.

Lara flipped the .45s, gripping them by the barrels to use as clubs, and slipped into a martial arts stance. The droid rained blows down on her, and Lara parried the droid's attempts with pistol butts and kicks.

As soon as Lara saw the droid's guard drop, she lashed out with a combat boot. The steel toe connected with the droid's right shoulder, spinning it around like a top.

As it turned, Lara leaped onto the droid's back, and ripped at a dented access plate. But it was no good—she couldn't get it off.

The droid flailed its arms, trying to reach her. The claws snapped within inches of Lara's flesh.

Drawing one of her sidearms, Lara aimed the .45 and fired it at the backplate. Shards of metal flew through the air. She holstered the .45, then reached inside the droid's exposed innards, closed her fingers on every wire she could grab, and yanked it all out.

Sparks exploded in the darkness. Abruptly, the droid powered down and collapsed.

Lara dropped to the floor and took the few steps to the shimmering disk. Even as her fingers closed on the prize, a razor-sharp claw slashed toward her face.

TWO

Croft Manor, England

Lara spun around and raised a hand. "Stop!"

Immediately, the droid froze.

Cautiously, Lara came closer, then leaned down and touched a panel on its chest. In response, a CD tray slid out that held a disk labeled KILL LARA CROFT. She switched the disk out for the one she'd gotten in the maze's center. This one was labeled: LARA'S PARTY MIX.

Instantly, the huge room was filled with throbbing music. The LEDs on the battered droid's graphic equalizer jumped and jerked to the hard driving rhythm.

Klieg lights suddenly flared to life and revealed the immense expanse of the grand ballroom filled with statues and idols.

Lara turned and glanced at the end of the room opposite the Grand Staircase that led to the upper floors. Glass walls glinted in ornate archways, enclosing a room filled with cutting-edge computer equipment. At the center of that cybernetic kingdom, Lara's friend and gadget whiz, Bryce Turing, sat before a cluster of monitors filled with attacking aircraft.

More than a little angry, Lara grabbed one of the droid's legs and dragged it toward Bryce's control room.

Bryce noticed the droid falling at his feet. He dropped beside the droid and ran his hands over it, fingering every ding and bullet hole. "For the love of Pete, Lara! Live rounds?"

Lara rolled a painful kink from her shoulder, then fixed Bryce with an icy stare. "Was the drill programmed to stop?"

Bryce hesitated. "Ah, that would be *no*. But you said it had to be challenging."

Lara nodded as if in agreement. "Yes. Hence the live fire."

Hillary entered the computer cubicle unannounced, carrying crisp white towels. The butler's eyes rested on a line of bullet holes. "Live rounds *again?*"

Showered and refreshed, rid of the powdered dust that had covered the ballroom floor, Lara emerged from her bathroom and found Hillary arranging blue flowers in a vase on the vanity her father had given her when she was a small girl.

Suits me. Lara crossed the elegant and spacious bedroom filled with antique furniture to the walk-in closet and pulled open the double doors. Inside, a lone, incredibly beautiful floral-print dress hung from the rod. All the rest of her clothes were missing.

Lara glared at Hillary over her shoulder. She hated to wear dresses. "Very funny."

Wisely, Hillary refrained from saying anything.

✿   ✿   ✿

Lara sat behind the huge desk in the study, her boots resting comfortably on the desk's edge. She gazed over the rest of the room, looking at the sheets covering the antique chairs and the sofa and the large globe. The shelves were filled with rare editions, illustrated manuscripts, and knick-knacks from around the world. If each one of those things was given the gift of speech, Lara knew that every item would have a story of derring-do and adventure to tell.

They were her father's adventures, and he'd shared some of them with her. However, Lord Croft had perished before he'd been able to tell them all.

Footsteps outside the study door alerted Lara of someone's arrival.

Hillary stepped cautiously into the room carrying an armload of files that contained projects for which people were requesting the Tomb Raider's help. "What are you doing in here?"

Retrieving and opening the file, Lara quickly flipped through the pictures inside. All of them showed a pyramid in a desert. "I don't want to go to Egypt again. Pyramids. Sand." She tossed the folder to the desk.

"I know. Gets everywhere. In the cracks." Hillary switched projects. "Spanish galleon?"

"To photograph or plunder?"

"Either. Perhaps both."

Reluctantly, Lara accepted the folder and leafed through it. "Do you know what day it is today, Hillary?"

"Yes. Of course. The fifteenth."

Lara tossed the Spanish galleon file on top of the pyramid one, rejecting it. "And that's never a good day."

She glanced over at the huge oil painting of a man in

khaki explorer's gear, very much the rugged adventurer. He stood in front of a tent flying the British Union Jack. The flag was frozen in mid-flutter. The inscription below the painting read:

LORD CROFT
1917–1985

"Never a good day," Hillary repeated sadly.

The last red rays of the setting sun blanketed the rose garden behind the manor house proper. The roses were in vigorous bloom and pollen made the air heavy. Crafted of marble, a field tent that was the exact replica of the one in her father's picture occupied the garden as its centerpiece.

Lara stood silently in front of the marble tent, clutching a single rose. It looked as though her father had just stepped out and would be back at any moment. A small headstone stood up from the ground slightly in front of the tent.

" 'To see a world in a grain of sand,' " Lara whispered, "and a heaven in a wild flower. . . ." Her voice thickened. "Miss you, Daddy." She moved forward then and knelt in front of the headstone. Tenderly, she laid the flower at the foot of the headstone.

LORD CROFT
DIED IN THE FIELD 15TH MAY, 1985
LOST BUT NEVER FORGOTTEN

THREE

Croft Manor, England

Lara watched the heavens through the large telescope in the manor house's Observatory. The Observatory was small and neat. The glass domed ceiling let in the moonlight. She sat in the chair behind the big telescope and watched Mercury and Venus, a blue and green light respectively, slowly approach alignment to the right of the moon.

"Don't get cold," Hillary chided her as he came up the spiral staircase from the large library below carrying a thick woolen blanket.

"Daddy would have loved this," she said. She turned, feeling momentarily lighter of heart, and reached out to touch part of the large brass model to her right. The suspended orrery depicted the solar system—the sun and all nine known planets—in all its glory.

Hillary draped the blanket over Lara's shoulders.

Lara pointed to the orrery. "Tonight, Pluto and Neptune align with Uranus. It's the first stage in the alignment of all nine planets, culminating in a full solar eclipse. It only happens once every five thousand years."

"When is the eclipse?" Hillary asked.

"Not until the eighteenth. But there's plenty to look out for until then. Some strange things are going to happen."

Something flared in the sky on the other side of the glass dome.

"What's that?" Hillary asked.

Lara saw more flashes as she studied the sky. A spiraling flash of light ignited, followed by a wisp of bright color. Arcs shot across the sky, followed by more that burned even brighter. "The Aurora Borealis. Like I said, strange things."

"Aurora," Hillary said, trying out the term, "Bor-e-al-is."

"The Northern Lights." Lara watched the lights play against the dark sky. They glittered like jewels. "Only way, way south. They normally only appear over the Pole."

"Good heavens. It's beautiful."

"It's *incredible*," Lara said, smiling. "Daddy *really* would have loved this." She watched a shower of meteors hammer through the blazing lights, vanishing quickly.

Lara slept fitfully, twisting and turning in the sheets. In the dream, she walked through the rose garden at night. Pale moonlight bathed the plants and the tent.

Golden light glowed inside the tent, painting the walls with their glow. As she approached the tent, the marble walls subtly shifted, becoming canvas that shivered in the thin breeze.

She reached for the fluttering tent flap and pulled it open. Shock trapped her breath at the back of her throat as she recognized who was inside the tent.

Her father sat on a stool before a folding field table. He adjusted the flame on a kerosene lamp, turning it brighter.

Lara remembered when she was seven and had been sitting in a tent just like the one in her dream. She'd been sitting cross-legged in the tent, watching her father writing an entry in one of his journals.

"What was that, Daddy?" she'd asked, referring to the flap of the canvas.

Her father had smiled. "Just the wind, Lara." He leaned toward her. "Look." He reached behind her left ear, and a pocket watch was suddenly in his hand. "The magic clock. Hidden for centuries just behind Lara's ear."

"Really?" Lara remembered the warm metal of the pocket watch in her hands when her father handed the device to her. She held it and listened to it ticking. . . .

. . . a ticking noise roused Lara for just a moment, then she went back to sleep.

In her dream, Lara opened the pocket watch and saw the black-and-white picture of her mother inside. "Mummy," she'd cried in delight.

"Yes," Lord Croft had replied.

"She looks so beautiful."

"She loved you very much, when you were just a teeny tiny baby." Her father had paused, looking at her as she looked at her mother. "I wish you could remember her."

"That's okay, Daddy. I have you."

"Yes, you do."

Lara had put the pocket watch to her ear. "And time. I have time."

"Rivers of time."

As the watch ticked almost methodically in her ear, the canvas had flapped again, but that time Lara had known what it was. "It's just the wind."

Lara remembered how she'd watched her father rise from the table and walk outside, leaving her alone in the tent.

That had been memory, Lara realized, but in the dream now she was sitting inside the tent. She sat beside the table where she'd sat as a little girl and the kerosene lantern flickered from the breeze invading the tent.

"Daddy? Is anybody out there?" She felt certain someone was watching. She raised her voice. "Daddy?"

She remembered she'd gone out into the night back then as well, stepping into the inky blackness and crying out after her father. "Daddy?"

Without warning, the tent flaps slapped shut, sealing her inside the canvas-shrouded prison.

Lara sat bolt upright in bed. "Daddy!"

Nothing—no one—was there.

She leaned back against her pillows, and it was only then that she noticed the *tick-tick-ticking* sound that floated up from somewhere in the house below. *That is definitely real.*

Tick . . . tick . . . tick . . . tick . . .

She followed the noise down the Grand Staircase. At the bottom of the staircase, she moved forward, intent on the steady noise. Only it wasn't ahead of her—it was *behind* her.

Lara turned and tracked the noise to the space beneath the staircase. She searched the paneling for a door. There was none.

She took a step away and kicked, shattering the paneling. A few quick heaves pulled the paneling free with short shrieks. She entered the dark area under the stairs. The ticking suddenly sounded louder.

A crate sat lodged under the low end of the staircase, covered with a thick layer of dust. Lara knelt and wiped the dust from the shipping label. It read:

CROFT/MISCELLANEOUS '81

A nearby shelf held several tools. She selected a flat-head screwdriver from the bunch and shoved it under the crate lid to loosen the covering. She lifted the lid to uncover her prize.

"Bryce!"

Reaching in his bed, Bryce grabbed his pillow and folded it over his head. He was certain the voice had to be part of some hideous nightmare he was having.

"Bryce!" This time the voice was followed by a horrid thumping noise.

Recognizing the sound as a fist banging against the door of his trailer, Bryce uncovered his head and glared across his room. Lara never willingly came banging on his door.

Skittering noises drew his attention, and he glanced down at the robotic bugs that inhabited the silver Airstream trailer that was his domicile as well. He'd forged the cyber-insects from spare parts for company.

"Hello, fellas," Bryce greeted them. He felt like death itself. "How's business?"

"Bryce!"

With a groan of effort, Bryce crossed over to the door just as another flurry of impatient blows rattled it in its hinges. He swung the door open and found Lara standing on the tiny, ramshackle metal steps that folded out away from the trailer.

"Why don't you live in the house?" Lara asked. "I have eighty-three rooms."

"I'm a free spirit, me."

Lara glanced at the trailer's tires, which were flat and sunk deeply into the mud. "Got it," she told him dryly. Then she turned and started marching back up the hill to the manor house.

Puzzled, Bryce watched after her. Obviously, she expected him to follow her. He looked around, surprised to find the light coming from the east. And his nose itched. "What's that smell?"

Lara answered without turning around. "It's six A.M."

"Oh," Bryce said, "this had better be good."

FOUR

Croft Manor, England

Lara studied the ornate antique clock that sat on one of the metal workbenches in Bryce's computer room. The clock was as big as a shoebox and ticked loudly.

Bryce lounged in his chair and sighed. "It's a clock."

"I found it last night," Lara said. "It was ticking."

"One of them *ticking* clocks, eh?"

"It was hidden in a secret room."

"Ooooh," Bryce said, raising his eyebrows like he was totally entranced by the story.

"Please," she said, not amused at all. "Don't even start."

"Lara. It's a clock. It ticks. It tells the time." Bryce checked his watch. "It's wrong."

"It *started* ticking," Lara pointed out. "Last night during the first stage of the alignment." She locked eyes with Bryce. "It woke me up."

The computer specialist took a deep breath and let it out slowly. He nodded. "Is anybody making any coffee?"

Lara studied the image on the computer monitor in front of her. The inner workings of the clock looked gigantic, magnified by the fiber-optic camera Bryce snaked through the guts of the antique timepiece.

"Looks pretty ordinary to me," Bryce observed.

Lara kept her attention on the monitor. "Keep looking."

Hillary arrived with a silver coffee service. He placed one of the big mugs next to Lara, then handed the other to Bryce. "Your coffee. Decaf latte with nonfat milk."

Bryce's attention shifted to Hillary. "Eh?"

Hillary grimaced. "What do you think?"

Bryce looked at the thick, hot, black liquid in the cup. He grinned. "Champion. Steaming sump oil. Ta." He released the fiber-optic cable.

Lara watched as the camera's viewpoint stuttered. The corner of a triangle, partially covered by the cogs and gears in the way, stood out immediately.

"Wait!" Lara said. "What did you do?"

"What did *I* do?"

Lara pointed at the triangle corner. "Where's that?"

Bryce shrugged. "I dunno. I just took my hands off the fiber-optic."

Lara traced the symbol with a finger. "Look at that."

"What is it?" Bryce asked. Hillary stepped in close behind him.

"I think—" Lara began.

Bryce shifted the fiber-optic slightly, but the corner of the triangle disappeared. "Bugger."

"Bugger," Lara agreed.

Bryce took out a small tool set he used on the inner workings of the computers. With slow, precise care, he opened the clock's housing to reveal the complicated mechanism inside. As he took out each screw, he carefully arranged it in the geometric progression he made.

Hillary rolled his eyes at the care the computer specialist was using.

Bryce glared at the other man. "That's my *map*, see. So I know where they all came from."

Why did it start ticking last night? Lara wondered. *And what am I supposed to find?* Her father never left things undone for her without expecting her to learn something from the experience. Surely, though, he'd taken his daughter's own impatient nature into account. He couldn't have expected her to take the clock apart piece by piece, and—

"It's all *camouflage*," Lara announced, interrupting the sound of the ticking clock for the first time in nearly half an hour.

Bryce looked up from his work, clearly not understanding. "What? Camouflage?"

Lara stood and crossed the room. She seized the greatly reduced clock in one hand. "Try this." She swung the clock against the metal workbench with all her strength. Metal pieces, cogs and springs, and delicate housing shattered loose and dropped to the floor. She seized a hammer and renewed her attack. Metal crumpled and tore, but it also gave way.

"O-kay," Bryce said, somewhat less than enthusiastic.

After a few more resounding *thwacks!,* Lara let go the hammer and picked up the battered clock. Within the space of a moment, she'd knocked off a great deal of the housing layers. She peered into the clock intently.

An opalescent eye peered back from the clock's interior. A raised cog pierced the center of the strangely glowing pupil.

More carefully now, Lara peeled away the last housing to reveal the inner core of the clock. Inside the clock was yet another clock, but this one appeared ancient.

"I see," Bryce said. "Hidden within. What is it?"

Hillary took down a digital camera from one of the cabinets. He switched the camera on and started taking picture after picture.

Hypnotized, pulled by the eye's beauty and meaning, Lara ran a fingertip over it. Then she began telling them the story of the Eye, remembering how her father had told her.

FIVE

Twenty Years Ago

"The All-Seeing Eye." Lord Croft held his thumbs and forefingers together to make the triangle that he peered through. The canvas walls of the field tent shimmered around them. Outside, the night remained silent.

Lara sat on the floor before her father, clinging to every word in little-girl fascination. She brought her hands up, imitating the triangle he made with her own thumbs and forefingers. Only she couldn't do it.

Before she grew frustrated, her father helped her place her fingers and thumbs correctly. Then they looked at each other through their own triangles.

"I see all," her father declared.

Stifling a giggle, Lara made her own voice deep. "I see *all*."

Her father reached into his jacket and brought out a cigar match. He struck the match and dragged it through the air while the head flared. "Long, long ago," he began, "a meteor crashed to Earth."

Earlier that day, Lara had seen some pictures in her father's old books. One of those pictures had been of a flaming meteor streaking across the sky.

"Strange phenomena began to occur around its crater." A beautiful painting had shown an ancient people dressed in leathers standing around the meteor crater. "An ancient people excavated the meteor and found, buried at its core, a mysterious, crystallized metal."

"A crystallized metal?" Lara repeated.

Another illustration showed a metal slab surrounded by the ancient people bowing in concentric circles around it. Sparks shot from the metal.

"They worshiped the metal for its magical powers," Lord Croft continued, "forging it into a sacred shape." He put his thumbs and forefingers together again. "A perfect triangle. They engraved upon it an emblem of its great power."

Lara gazed in wonder at the picture of the triangle in the journal. A great eye stared out of its center.

"The mysterious Triangle," her father continued, "gave its guardians great insights, great knowledge in mathematics and science."

Turning another page of her father's book, Lara studied the picture of the great city. A tall pyramid occupied the center of the city.

"They called themselves the People of the Light," her father said. "But others heard of the power of the Triangle and wanted it for themselves. And soon great war raged, and the People of the Light suffered under a terrible siege."

The next page showed a drawing of warriors standing along the outside walls of the city.

"As fire engulfed their homes," her father said, "the sun appeared to go out. It was, in fact, a total eclipse. Believing the end of the world to be upon them, their High Priest cried out to the heavens. 'Let our enemies be vanquished!' The High Priest held the Triangle in his hands before him, and it began to glow."

As he told the story, Lord Croft's brass orrery began to revolve, lining up the sun, the moon, and the planets.

"And with the words still on his lips," her father went on, "his prayers were answered in a horrific instant!"

Lara turned the page to an illustration of the eye atop the temple erupting in a blinding flash of light. Lara gazed at the images of the warriors scattered on the ground, horrified looks on their dead faces.

"Death was everywhere," her father said. "They later called it the Tomb of Ten Thousand Shadows. The High Priest then understood this power should not be held by any man. A power that could explode the human mind. The power of God."

The page Lara currently looked at showed the Triangle again, only now it had been sliced into two parts.

"The High Priest," Lord Croft said, "ordered the Triangle cut into two. One half was to stay at the temple, while the other half was to be hidden at the end of the Earth to prevent the Triangle's strange power from being used to change the fate of humankind."

❖   ❖   ❖

Drawn back to the present, Lara stared into the rapt faces of Bryce and Hillary.

"And?" Bryce asked.

"Well, children," Lara said, smiling, "that was by no means the end of the matter. In defiance of the High Priest, the craftsmen who had cut the Triangle in half secretly made a highly advanced clock to serve as a guide to find the hidden piece and preserve the Triangle's awesome powers for future generations of their kind. They called themselves the *Illuminati.*"

Seven-year-old Lara watched the brass globes spin on her father's orrery.

"They realized that the *exact* alignment of the planets necessary to activate the Triangle—" Lord Croft watched as the model spun to a stop in the nine-planet alignment, "—would not be due for another five thousand years." He reached into his jacket and took out an antique pocket watch. He let the timepiece dangle by its chain from his fingers and it slowly spun. "And that would prove to be just long enough for little Lara Croft to grow up and find it!"

Even though Lara was watching closely, she only saw her father's hand move briefly, then the pocket watch was gone. It was *magic*. She loved when he did magic.

Lord Croft grinned mischievously. "And now it's time to go to bed. With all this in your head, you should have wonderful dreams."

Lara stared at the clock that had been hidden within the ornate structure.

Bryce shook his head, mesmerized. "Okay. You got me. What now?"

Lara didn't answer. She turned and walked from the room, not having an answer for Bryce's question. At the moment, she had questions of her own and she knew where she could get some of them answered.

Dressed in black leather and dark shades, Lara threw a leg over the Norton Streetfighter. She sped by the other vehicles quartered in the garage. They ranged from a sporty little MG to a fully loaded Land Rover. Cars, after all, were tools and a kind of accessory.

Today Lara preferred the Norton. Astride the powerful motorcycle, she felt like an arrow fired from a bow.

She roared up the exit ramp and tripped the electronic garage door opener. When she shot through the entrance, she cleared the door by inches. She sped through the estate and through the large wrought-iron gates at the end. In less than a minute, she was on the road. At her present speed, London was only moments away.

"Lot 121 . . . a Louis XV ormolu-mounted bracket, showing on my left. One million, eight hundred thousand pounds . . . one million, nine hundred thousand . . ."

Lara arrived at the antiques auction in Boothby's Auction House well after the morning's business had started. The large auditorium held a sizable crowd made up of collectors, archaeologists, and lawyers.

The auctioneer at the head of the room continued describing the gilded mantel clock on the showcase table.

". . . two million-three, thank you," the auctioneer said,

acknowledging the discreet bidding. "Two million-four, thank you, sir."

A lady wearing an ornate, brocade dress fanned herself madly to Lara's left. It would have taken a trained eye to catch her in the act of bidding.

". . . two million, six hundred thousand. Any more at two million, six hundred thousand? . . . Sold," the auctioneer announced when no one offered to top the woman's last bid.

Lara glanced through the crowd, spotting Wilson, the man she'd come to London to see, when he walked up onto the auction stage to make the notation on the ormolu clock's tag. He was a thin man of advanced years, and one of Lord Croft's close friends.

Wilson caught Lara's eye and gave her a small nod. He turned and left the stage, disappearing in the corridor behind it.

"Next item," the auctioneer went on, "lot 122. The Dagger of Xian."

A pair of security guards strode up to the stage and placed the display case on the auction table. The jeweled dagger within the protective case gleamed like fire.

Lara got up and left the auction room. She followed the hallway around to the crowded lobby where buyers and sellers hustled each other.

"Lara Croft."

Lara knew that voice, and she'd halfway hoped that she'd never see the man again, all the while wishing that she would.

She turned.

SIX

Boothby's Auction House, London

Alex West strode through the crowded lobby, making straight for Lara. Alex was tall and rugged looking, thirty-ish. He looked out of place in the suit. "Still pretending to be a photojournalist?" he asked. "Y'know, it's cool that you still have a day job, even though it is obviously just for show. And how 'bout them Pulitzer Prizes?" He made his eyes large and round. "I mean—*wow.*"

Lara arched an eyebrow at him. "They seem to impress the little people. Still pretending to be an archaeologist, Alex?"

Alex frowned. "Hey, Lara, do we always have to fight like this? I mean, maybe we don't."

"Maybe we do," Lara said.

"Why?"

"Has *Tibet* slipped your mind?"

Alex rubbed a hand across the back of his neck and reddened slightly. "Ah—huh. The prayer wheels."

"Yes. I paid you in advance."

"Now that, uh, was a finder's fee."

"No, that was a *consulting* fee. I didn't ask you to *find* anything."

"What?"

"You *stole* my prayer wheels," Lara accused.

"Steal?" Alex glanced around hurriedly. "Me? From you? No. I mean, it's not like you ever really *owned* them or anything. You and me, babe: the same animal."

Lara met his gaze. "Oh, really." She smiled at him, then turned and walked away.

"Lara," he called.

Lara cut him off before he could speak, glancing back quickly at a group of Japanese collectors expectantly hovering around. "I think your clients need you."

When Alex glanced back, the Japanese group immediately made their way over to him.

"Lara," Alex tried again weakly.

"Run along." Lara grinned. "Mr. West, you're wanted on the floor. After all, as you once said, so memorably: it's all just a business."

Alex looked at her, but didn't have anything to say.

Lara waved good-bye, then turned at her name.

"Lara. Lara, my dear." Wilson hurried from the crowd, a smile filling his face.

"Mr. Wilson," Lara greeted, then embraced the man. "Good to see you."

Wilson glanced around the crowded lobby, then offered his arm. "Let's go to my study."

Clocks and clock mechanisms filled the shelves to overflowing in Wilson's study. Several of them ticked, creating different layers of noise. As Boothby's resident horologist, there was nothing about clocks that he didn't know.

"Lara," he said, "this is a very unique object." He turned the silver rod that pierced the glowing eye symbol in the clock. The casing opened and revealed the inner workings.

Lara joined him, looking again at the strange dials she had found back at Croft Manor. Inscriptions were etched into the metal around the dials. "Only one of the dials is working at the moment," she pointed out. "It glows like the eye. Less so, but it's getting brighter."

Wilson turned the clock over, looking more closely.

"And it seems to be running backward," Lara said, "like it's not so much keeping time, but *counting down* to something."

Wilson pointed at the tiny, intricate arrangement of cogs at the center of the clock face. "Yes. Yes. You see this? It reverses the direction of the action, so the outer clock face would run forward." He indicated the luminous dial with three small dot symbols orbiting it. "And these—"

"I thought they looked like planets," Lara ventured.

"Yes. They could very well be."

"The clock began ticking the night the first three planets aligned."

"Fascinating." Wilson's gaze lingered on the clock. "Incredible. Incredibly beautiful."

"And it's perfectly sealed," Lara said. "I don't know how. I can't find a seam. And I didn't want to break it."

Wilson turned back to the clock. "No. You shouldn't break a thing like this."

"Daddy *hid* it, Mr. Wilson. It was hidden in the house for twenty years."

"He must have thought it was very valuable."

"He surrounded it with other objects. Random stuff. Things that are highly valuable on the open market, but to a true insider, just trinkets. Baubles."

Wilson nodded.

"His field journals made no mention of the clock," she went on, "and the last one he was working on had half its pages ripped out."

"He always steered his own course, your father." Wilson placed the clock on his desk. "He was a great man." He paused for a moment, as if lost in memory. "Would you like some port? It's really very fine."

Lara shook her head.

Wilson's hand shook a little as he poured a single glass of wine. "I can't help you, Lara."

Lara glanced at Wilson. The possibility of that response had never entered her mind. "Mr. Wilson?"

"I mean, I have never seen anything like this. It's beyond my expertise. It truly is . . . a mystery." Wilson paused. "You should keep it for yourself."

Lara glanced back at the clock on Wilson's desk. Out of all the dozens of ticking clocks in the room, the one she'd found such a short while ago seemed the loudest of all. Not knowing what to say, she only nodded.

Hours after Lara Croft had left his study, Wilson sat behind his desk. His cheeks were wet with the tears he'd shed in that time. He held a picture of himse;f with Lord Croft. "Forgive me." He picked up the phone and dialed.

It was answered almost at once.

"Lara? Yes. Well, ah, you see, I had a second thought about that clock. There *is* a man who may be able to help you. A friend of mine. I told him about the, ah, the clock and he's very intrigued. He may be able to help identify its origin."

The next morning, Lara parked her car before the tall townhouse at the address Wilson had given her. She wore black trousers, a tank top, and a full-length coat against the morning's chill. She also had her backpack. As she went up the short flight of stairs to the town house, she studied the featureless black door. Wilson had offered no explanation about what Powell's occupation was, and the door gave absolutely no indication.

The black door opened before she reached it and a man stepped out. "Lady Croft?"

Lara nodded. "Mr. Powell?"

The man smiled. "Oh, good heavens, no. No. I am his associate, Mr. Pimms."

"Mr. Pimms?"

"Yes," Pimms said agreeably. "Like the beverage." He turned and led Lara up the steps and into the town house.

Inside the lobby, a man was carefully restoring an ancient bust.

Pimms led Lara around the sculpture. "A painstaking process," the man said. "Very skilled, I'm told."

Lara studied the bust in passing, fascinated by the process. "Who is it?"

Pimms paused for just a moment to regard the sculpture. "Ah, you know, I'm not actually sure."

Lara smiled back, then resumed following him through the house. They journeyed through a grand vestibule stocked with striking statues and art that she recognized as products from North Africa and Asia.

"What does Mr. Powell *do*?" she asked Pimms.

"He's a lawyer," Pimms replied.

"Isn't it obvious?" a man's voice boomed.

SEVEN

London, England

Turning, Lara watched the man approach. He wore a smoking jacket, a long gown, and a fez. He offered her a broad, confident smile, then extended his hand.

"Lady Croft," he said. "My pleasure. Manfred Powell, Q.C."

Lara took his hand. "Mr. Powell. Good morning."

"Lady Croft was wondering whose was the face in the restoration," Pimms said.

"Pluto," Powell said. "Not the dog, you understand, but the King of the Underworld."

"Right," Lara said.

Powell led them into a small study off the vestibule. It was ornate, definitely a man's room—it smelled of cigars—and housed more antiquities. "But of course, I know you know the difference, Lady Croft. I believe you are quite an authority on things ancient and mythological." He waved her to a chair in front of the massive Louis XIV desk.

Pimms remained standing.

"Well," Lara said, "you know. I travel."

Powell steepled his fingers and gazed across them at her. "Mr. Wilson said you were quite the archaeologist."

"He's very sweet."

"He knew your father, I believe."

"They were great friends."

Powell smiled. "Wonderful. I had the honor of meeting him myself once. In Venice." He glanced up over Lara's shoulder. "Of course, Mr. Pimms. I forgot you had to get going."

"Ah, yes," Pimms said. "Of course."

Lara glanced over her shoulder at the younger man. He seemed a little disappointed.

Powell lifted an eyebrow. Without another word, Pimms left the room. Powell turned his attention back to Lara.

Lara opened her backpack, noticing the lawyer's eager interest. Disappointment flattened his smile a little when he saw that she had only brought 8 × 10 glossy pictures of the clock. Wilson's odd behavior, despite his long association with her father, had rung too many warning bells. The clock was safely locked up at the manor house.

"Very interesting," Powell said. "The All-Seeing Eye. It's a shame you only brought photographs."

She passed them across the desk.

Powell carefully spread the pictures out across the desktop. He retrieved a magnifying glass from a desk drawer and began inspecting them.

Lara watched him carefully inspect the images of the clock and its intricate dials.

"Nevertheless," Powell said, "it *is* fascinating. You said it started ticking the night of the Aurora?"

"Yes." Lara decided to be close-mouthed about the clock. She had the impression that he knew more about the clock than he was saying, and probably more than she did.

"Hmmm," Powell mused.

Lara waited a moment, then asked, "Have you ever heard of the 'Clock of the Ages'? "

"Hmmmm?" Powell didn't look up. "No. But it sounds intriguing. You must tell me about it."

Lara shrugged. "It's a myth. An ancient clock that is a map, and a key. Actually."

"To a buried treasure, no doubt."

The ivory-handled letter opener caught Lara's eye. There, nearly at the end of it, was a tiny crest that showed an eye trapped within a triangle: the All-Seeing Eye.

"You said you were a lawyer?" Lara asked casually.

"Yes."

"And this," Lara said, gesturing to her photos, "this is a hobby?"

Powell smiled slightly. "This is an *obsession*. And really my specialty. My practice centers around antiquities."

"I see." Lara wasn't convinced at all.

Powell put his magnifying glass down on the photos and sat back in his chair. "But this . . . completely eludes me. I think I have never seen anything quite so beautiful that I know so little about."

Lara smiled because it was expected. "That's *it?*"

"A wise man knows what he doesn't know," Powell said.

"And admits as much," Lara finished.

Powell nodded. "Exactly." He stood, signaling that the meeting was over. He held up a print. "And this is pleasurable torment. My ignorance amuses me."

Lara stood as well and inclined her head, taking her leave. *You,* she thought, *are a skilled liar, but a liar nonetheless.*

" 'My ignorance amuses me'? " Bryce repeated.

"That's what he said." Lara was on the other side of the Tech Room hauling an old cardboard box onto a bench.

Bryce held a magnifying glass to one of the photographs Lara had shown Powell. "My ignorance amuses me, too."

"Yes. I've always found your ignorance amusing. But Powell's not ignorant."

"No?"

Lara sliced through the packing tape on the cardboard box, then opened it. "No. He's lying. He knows a lot more than he is letting on. Something's *up* with Mr. Powell." She took an old record turntable from the box.

"What is that?" Bryce asked.

"Inspiration," Lara replied.

EIGHT

Croft Manor, England

Lara carefully wiped the soft cloth across the surface of the vinyl record. Then she placed it tenderly on the turntable and lifted the needle over to it. Soft music filled the ballroom. She strode up the Grand Staircase and met Hillary at the first landing.

"Is there anything you need?" Hillary asked.

"No, thank you, Hilly," Lara answered. "Go to bed."

"I will. Don't you stay up too late."

Lara checked the cinch on the bungee cord harness that attached her to the lines hanging from the high ceiling. Then she leaped over the side. The floor was twenty feet below and coming up fast. She executed a double flip, spotting Hillary heading up the stairs to bed while she hurtled toward the floor.

The bungee lines pulled taut and slowed her fall, then yanked her back up. She double-flipped again at the apex of the jump, then fell again. The music crescendoed throughout the manor house.

Movement caught her eyes on the way back down the second time. Shadows flitted out on the estate grounds, running toward the main house. She'd just reached the bottom of her jump when she noticed the ruby laser sights sweeping in controlled rhythm across the lobby outside the Grand Ballroom.

They're already in the house. Lara vaulted back up toward the ceiling, altering her trajectory so she could reach out and snag the support line of the huge chandelier hanging from the center of the room. Crystal rattled, making a cacophony of tinkling, but she held on. She started swinging her body around and around to gain momentum, then flung herself toward the staircase railing.

Sure-footed as a panther, Lara landed on the railing. Aided by the bungee cords, she managed to run straight up the railing, defying gravity. When she reached the limit of the bungee cords, she unclipped them from her belt but remained a few yards short of the balcony above. She gathered herself, knowing she was risking a long fall if she missed, and leaped.

She arched her body, twisting and moving like a gymnast to get the most from her effort. Then she landed on the balcony. She paused only for a moment, heard the crash of breaking glass below as the shadows kicked in the windows, then ran along the upper corridor.

As the assault team filled the Grand Ballroom below, Lara raced around the circular landing above. The men wore black assault gear, night-vision goggles, and carried military weapons. The ruby laser sights filled the manor house, then a couple flicked across her, tracking her. Without warning, a line of bullet holes crashed into the wall behind her just as she raced past. Plaster dust swirled out into the air. The assault team had to be using silencers because there was very little noise.

Two attackers reached the top of the stairwell opposite Lara's position. They opened fire as she ducked into a long passageway. She hugged the wall for protection, but knew they'd be after her in heartbeats. Laser sights suddenly danced down the hallway with her.

Moving quickly, Lara opened a closet door, grimly aware that it would be reduced to splinters almost immediately and provided very little cover. She threw her body against the next door she came to, ripping the door from the hinges and tumbling inside. Bullets tore the doorframe to pieces.

Lara gazed wildly across the room, spotting the doors of the dumbwaiter on the wall. As she ran across the room, she heard the motion detector alarms trip.

"Intruder alert," the booming mechanical voice announced. "Intruder alert—Tech Room."

My clock, Lara realized as she opened the dumbwaiter doors and crawled inside. She closed them behind her. The Tech Room was where she'd left the clock. She sat on the dumbwaiter and hoisted herself down, a partial plan already in mind. Whoever had sent these men had seriously misjudged her.

As she went down the dumbwaiter shaft, her watch peeped. She shut it off and kept going hand-over-hand. At the bottom of the shaft, she kicked the doors open and leaped out. She went halfway down the wall in the dark room and found the light switch. When she turned it on, light filled the Equipment Room.

Her vehicles waited in sedate lines, carefully organized with each in its place. She turned to the right, spotting the large weapons vault locked up tight against the wall, the weapons visible through the glass.

She ran to the weapons vault and started punching in the security code. Before she could finish, a deafening explosion hammered the door only a few feet away.

The door buckled, blown in by the explosives. Three assassins followed it inward, leveling their weapons at once and sweeping the room. Ruby lights flickered over Lara, then bullets filled the air.

Having no choice, she retreated, jumping and flipping as bullets rent the air around her and scarred the concrete floor. She kept moving, only a heartbeat ahead of death.

Bryce slammed all his weight against the trailer's door again, but only succeeded in enlarging the bruised area on his shoulder. The intruder alert squalling from the Tech Room, relayed through his own computer systems, had woken him first, then he'd made out the sounds of destruction reverberating throughout the manor house.

He knew he was no hero, hadn't signed on to be one, but he wasn't about to leave Lara alone to face whoever was invading the estate. He slammed his body against the door again and screamed in pain. *They locked me in!* he suddenly realized. There could be no other answer. He cursed, but that didn't do any good, either.

But it did draw the attention of at least one guard posted outside the trailer. Two bullets punched holes through the thin trailer wall, leaving ripped metal and splintered wood in their wake.

Bryce ducked as a third round cut through the door and angled up through the roof. He glanced wildly around the room and spotted the laptop on the desk. All of his computers were tied into the manor house; all of them had access. He grabbed the laptop and crawled under the desk.

"Come on, boyo," Bryce entreated. "Come on."

The monitor flickered, then showed the view from one of the security cameras inside the Grand Ballroom. Bryce changed the angle and zoomed in on the droid, propped up against one wall. He'd worked on it the last couple of days, repairing the damage Lara had done to it, but the repairs weren't complete.

Sparks sizzled from the droid and it shivered. But it couldn't get up. Bryce hit the command keys again, but the mass of metal just sparked and shorted out.

The window on the computer monitor that showed the droid's on-line status suddenly went black. A moment later, CONSULT YOUR DEALER! appeared across the screen.

Lara took cover behind a massive steel chest. The three men in the Equipment Room with her had evidently decided not to take chances. They hung back warily, but kept up the heavy fire from the assault rifles.

She kicked her feet through the debris. All of it was communications gear that had been stacked neatly on shelves that were now being smashed by flying bullets. She spotted a com-link headset, consisting of a pencil mike and an earpiece, and picked it up. When she put it on, she was surprised to find it was still operational.

"Bryce," she called, switching to the frequency they always used inside the house. *"Bryce! Come in!"* She risked a glance around the metal chest, knowing it wouldn't take long for the three men to get their nerve up. If they rushed her—

"Bryce! I'm in the Equipment Room."

Hearing Lara's voice galvanized Bryce into action. He couldn't believe it, couldn't believe she was still alive or had found a way to get in touch with him.

He snatched his com-link headset from his desk. He pulled it on and clicked through the security camera menu in the house, quickly bringing up the feed there. He tapped the mike and let her know he was there.

Lara crouched with her back to the metal chest as she stripped the canvas bag from the prize inside. The wide-snouted 38mm grenade launcher looked blunt and ugly. A dozen or so grenades lay inside. However, instead of explosive rounds, the grenades only contained tear gas.

Then the lights in the room started going out. Lara knew the three men had found the light control panel and intended to make good use of their night-vision goggles. In seconds, she was sitting in darkness, the grenade launcher armed and resting across her knees.

"Switch to night vision, Bryce," Lara instructed. For the moment, her attackers had ceased firing. "You have to be my eyes."

"Are you armed?" Bryce asked over the com-link.

Lara racked the grenade launcher. "After a fashion."

"Do you have a mask?" Bryce asked.

"I'm *improvising*." Lara jerked a thumb over her shoulder. "Talk to me. They're stealing my bloody clock."

Bryce brought up the pull-down menu for the security cameras inside the manor house and quickly opened a window that showed the Tech Room where the clock was kept. The alarms had lowered the steel cage over the sensitive areas as they were supposed to do, but the invaders had brought along acetylene torches. The harsh flames cut through the steel bars.

He switched back to the equipment room and blinked as the night vision showed the large room in a stunning array of greens. The four people inside the room glowed brightest of all, and the laser targeting beams on the assault rifles were a close second.

"Right," Bryce said into the microphone. "Three bad guys. All night-vision equipped. Number one is standing by the Aston Martin."

Lara started to move even as the assassin locked into position. Bryce just knew he was about to see Lara cut to ribbons by a hail of bullets!

NINE

Croft Manor, England

Lara mentally fixed the man's position in her mind, using the muzzle flashes as a reference. She pushed herself up, leveled the grenade launcher, and stroked the trigger. The launcher bucked in her arms.

The 38mm round sped across the room and smashed against the assassin's Kevlar-covered chest, knocking him back ten yards against the wall. He didn't get back up.

"Bingo!" Bryce reported enthusiastically.

Lara didn't feel quite so enthusiastic. It wouldn't be long before she was in danger of being overcome by the gas herself. "Next."

"Number two, crouching, by the TVR."

Lara pictured the sports car's location. She popped up

from hiding and fired. She heard the sound of breaking glass but no meaty thud. She'd missed.

"Sorry," Bryce apologized. "I reparked the TVR."

Lara ducked and a barrage of shots rocked the metal crate. She broke the launcher open and fed in another round. "You drove my TVR?"

"Well, I just ran it into the village for—"

"Later!"

"Number two's moving to the Lotus. He's standing."

The first of the tear gas reached Lara then, burning and tightening her lungs and nasal passages, making her cough. She leaned over the metal crate and fired. This time there was a resounding thud of flesh being properly pounded.

Despite her coughing fit, Lara smiled in satisfaction. She dashed from the metal crate toward the wall. A pegboard hung there, covered with keys to all the vehicles in the garage.

As fast as she could, Lara pressed all the ignition buttons, listening as the engine on each vehicle caught. The garage filled with the thundering rumble of high-performance engines. A coughing fit overcame Lara for a moment, but she forced herself to keep going.

"Number three's hiding between the MacLaren and your dad's old Lea Francis," Bryce announced.

Lara moved through the shadows. "Hiding?"

"He's pretty upset. I think he might run his keys down the side of the MacLaren."

By feel, wracked by coughing from the tear gas, Lara located the MacLaren's distinctive key fob. She pressed the button as she leaned out from cover.

The MacLaren's lights flared to life, catching the assassin in their glare. The sudden light temporarily blinded him through the night-vision goggles.

Lara launched herself at the man immediately, abandoning the grenade launcher because she didn't want any more gas released in the room. She flipped into a handstand, then kicked out with both feet, catching the man in the head. The assassin flew back, unconscious before he collapsed to the ground.

Bryce groaned in appreciation. "Oh, you're *done,* mate."

Still in motion, Lara breathed shallowly, her eyes tearing now, and ran for the weapons vault. She retrieved the grenade launcher and used it to smash through the security glass, then reached inside to get her twin .45s.

She ran out into the hallway leading back up into the manor house, her pistols ready in both hands. In seconds she was back in the Grand Ballroom, staring at the ruin of the Tech Room.

The steel cage gaped, showing several bars missing, ending in blackened stumps. The clock was gone. So were the men who'd taken it.

Manfred Powell knelt on a rice mat in his office. Powell wore a black robe and meditated. A brushed steel orrery was spinning nearby. The men he'd sent out to the Croft mansion had returned only moments ago.

And they'd brought the clock with them.

A timid knock sounded at the door.

"Go away," Powell ordered.

In an unusual act of defiance, Pimms entered the room just as the orrery came to a stop. "Good morning." Then he saw the clock sitting on the desk and his eyes went wide. "Is that the clock?"

"No," Powell replied sarcastically, "it's a fish I caught. It's a bouquet of fresh-cut flowers."

"I see." Pimms seemed chastised.

Powell stood in one fluid move.

"Did . . . is, ah, Lady Croft, ah . . . dead?" Pimms asked quietly.

"No," Powell replied, taking a cup of green tea from the service on the tray beside his desk. "Still in the game."

"Wonderful." Pimms halted his sigh of relief when he caught a look from Powell. "Good, I mean."

"Girl's clearly got a lot of spunk."

"Yes. Well. She's very . . . ah . . ."

"She taught my men a thing or two about home invasion. I'm sure we'll see her again."

"You think so?" Pimms asked.

Powell smiled. "We may even need to hire her." He drained his cup of tea.

Pimms approached the clock. "Can I?"

"Look with your eyes," Powell told him.

Pimms drew his hand back. "Of course. It's very beautiful. Ingenious. What makes it glow?"

"A previously revoked law of Nature."

Powell sat at his desk and studied the astronomical charts that he brought up on his laptop computer. He referred to the clock, the orrery and a sextant as he worked through the information he deciphered and translated.

Pimms's eyes hadn't left the clock. "And this can lead us to the first tomb? What are you going to tell the High Council?"

"That we figured it out with our very expensive super-computers," Powell replied.

Pimms frowned. "We did?"

Irritated, Powell closed his laptop. "No. We did not. We failed utterly. But we are not about to admit it."

"No?" Pimms asked. "I mean—no. Of course not. We figured it out with our computers."

Powell smiled, like an owner would smile at a pet that had done a good trick. "That's the spirit, man. You're getting the hang of it. Lies and half-truths." His grinned widened. "Except, of course, when dealing with me."

"Right."

"Croft had it all these years."

"Lara Croft?" Pimms looked surprised.

"No." Powell's irritation returned. "Lord Croft. I doubted its existence but he felt it in his bones."

"He was a great man," Pimms said.

"Yes, he was," Powell agreed. "But then again, I'm alive and he's not."

Lara answered the door, after checking to make sure it was only the FedEx deliveryman and not some unsavory sort wanting to add insult to injury after last night's raid. She took the letter he offered, then signed the clipboard. She glanced at him, discovering him staring in awe at the bullet-riddled Grand Ballroom.

"I woke up one morning," Lara said casually, "and I just hated everything."

The FedEx guy ripped his copy from the package he'd handed her. He looked more than a little confused.

"Thanks." He turned and headed quickly back to his vehicle.

Bryce peered over Lara's shoulder as she closed the door. "Who's Stribling, Clive, and Winterset, then? Sounds like a bunch of lawyers."

Lara looked at him. "They're a bunch of lawyers."

"Oh. Shut my face again."

"Well, you are very nosy." Lara opened the envelope and found another envelope inside. A letter on Stribling, Clive, & Winterset stationery was attached to it, neatly typewritten. As she read it, Lara made her way to the broken Grand Staircase and sat down weakly.

As per instructions of our client, Lord Croft, enclosed letter to be delivered to his daughter, Lara, on the 6th day of July, 2001, if, and only if, client should pre-decease this date.

Hillary walked into the room and took in the gravity of the situation at once. His face showed concern. "Lara?"

"It's—" Lara was surprised to find her voice shaking. "It's a letter from my father."

"Your *father*?" Hillary repeated.

Lara nodded. "Written before he died and delivered today as per his instructions."

Forgetting his aplomb for once, Hillary cursed in surprise.

Calming herself, Lara studied the envelope she held. It was sealed with a red wax blob, the C seal of Lord Croft pressed into it. Only her name, *Lara,* was written across the front of the envelope in her father's elegant hand.

She took her pocketknife from her shorts and sliced through the red wax seal easily. When she opened the envelope, her hands shook slightly. And she read.

> *To see a World in a Grain of Sand,*
> *And a Heaven in a Wild Flower,*
> *Hold Infinity in the Palm of your Hand*
> *And Eternity in an Hour.*

The brevity of the note hurt Lara. Her father had sent her this note, intended to be delivered so long after his death, and yet . . . there was *so* little. She read through the words again, then she remembered where they were from.

She leaped from the staircase and ran into the Great Library. Swiftly, she grabbed the sliding ladder mounted onto the front of the shelves and swarmed up it.

Her father had collected thousands of books over the years, and had read every one of them. But there was a favorite that he had, and a favorite edition of it as well. Lara found it with ease and pulled it gently from the shelf. It was a first edition of *William Blake: Poetry.*

She turned and sat on the ladder, flipping through the pages. After only a moment, she found the poem she was looking for.

> *Auguries of Innocence*
> *To see a World in a Grain of Sand,*
> *And a Heaven in a Wild Flower,*
> *Hold Infinity in the Palm of your Hand*
> *And Eternity in an hour.*

Quietly, Lara read through the poem, coming to the last lines. " 'We are led to Believe a Lie/When we see not Thro' the Eye . . .'" She stared at the triangle drawn in black ink beside the text.

The illustration wasn't one of Blake's; her father had drawn it. Inside the triangle was an eye. Quickly, Lara flipped to the back of the book, finding the All-Seeing Eye embossed on it. She took out her pocketknife again and carefully sliced open the book's handmade binding.

She quoted the next lines of the poem from memory. " 'Which was Born in a Night to Perish in a Night/When the Soul Slept in Beams of Light.' "

Underneath the old leather was a letter and small clutch of notes. The papers were wafer-thin, covered in her father's tiny, neat script. Lara opened them.

> *My Darling Daughter,*
> *I knew you would figure this out . . .*

TEN

Croft Manor, Twenty Years Ago

Lord Croft sat at his desk in the Great Library and contemplated the last letter he would ever write to his daughter. He tried not to think of it that way, but there was no other way to think of it.

If you are reading this letter then I am no longer with you. And I miss you, and I love you always, and forever.

He gazed across the Library and watched Lara spinning the globe there. She was seven, only a child. Funny that he never really thought of that when he dragged her across the world, but thinking of her now—alone, without him— he realized how truly young she was. He turned back to his writing.

It also means I have failed, and must lay an awesome burden on your shoulders. For this I am deeply sorry.

The power of the Triangle is real, Lara. If its two pieces are reunited, its possessor will wield a God-like power which I have come to believe would be ruinous to Humankind.

The clock I told you about is the key to the location of its pieces, its precise latitude and longitude.

Feeling a rhythmic sensation against her combat boot, Lara glanced up from the notes her father had left concerning the Triangle and spotted one of Bryce's robotic insects crawling up the boot. They were in Bryce's trailer and the little creatures had full run of the trailer. Irritably, Lara kicked the robot bug away.

"Hey," Bryce protested.

Lara turned her attention to the keyboard in front of her and typed furiously. "It was crawling up my leg."

"*He* was crawling up your leg," Bryce corrected.

"*It*," Lara responded. She punched up a computer-generated model of the solar system. "I think I've got it." She pointed to the screen, waiting for Bryce to join her.

"O-kay," Bryce quipped.

"So we think the three dots on each dial of the clock represent planets, and the clock is ticking backward, right?"

"Right."

"The first three planets to align," she went on, "were Pluto, Neptune, and Uranus."

On-screen, the three named planets shifted into alignment.

"And then those three aligned, our clock started ticking. Right?"

"Right."

"Now." Lara took the image of the clock and scanned it into the computer. "The three planetary dots provide a basic starmap, a guide to latitude, and I'm sure these *symbols . . .*" She clicked the mouse again, bringing up another window with greater detail of the runic markings around each dial. ". . . are the key to some measurement of longitude." She returned the monitor to the solar system. "My father said the Triangle was divided into two. Now there are *two* more stages in the alignment."

"Two more dials on the clock," Bryce stated quietly.

"You're a genius," Lara said.

"I *am* a genius," Bryce declared in triumph. He exchanged high-fives with her.

"So here's the solar system, as of today, 17:28 GMT." Lara tapped another key. "Let's just speed everything up." She watched as the program ran faster. "And here goes Saturn, Jupiter, and Mars. Just at that exact second the second dial of our ticking clock reaches zero."

Bryce read the information with her. "In forty-eight hours."

Lara pushed up from the desk. She had equipment to get, then to figure out a way to get where she was going.

In a few days I leave for a long journey, which I hope will lead me to the Clock. If I do not find it, I fear there are others who will. And these are dangerous men.

I believe I have deduced the secret location of the

*Tomb of the Dancing Light, where the first half of the
Triangle is hidden. I may be wrong, but God willing,
I am not. However, I cannot test my theory as each
piece of the Triangle is hidden not only in* space *but
also in* time.

He paused again, stretching his hand, which had gotten
tight with effort. Lara was back at the globe, spinning it.
He'd given her a problem to solve, one that was linked
with the letter he was now writing.

"Did you find it yet?" he asked.

Lara smiled at him. "I found it ages ago, but you were
still writing, Daddy. So I was just spinning it."

"Ah, yes. Keep things moving." That was Lara's whole
attitude, but she'd come by it quite honestly.

*Whatever happens to me, whether I get the clock
for you or not, you must be in the Tomb of the Dancing Light at the exact moment of the planetary alignment.*

*Even in this letter I only dare reveal the merest
clue to its whereabouts, so high are the stakes in-
volved in this enterprise.*

Lord Croft crossed the Library to join his young daughter. She reached out and stopped the big globe in her little
hands.

"There it is." She traced her forefinger across Asia, closing in on her target. "The Khmer Kingdom."

"Yes," Lord Croft responded, "Cambodia, very good."
He captured her hand in his, then guided her finger to a

point on the map that was marked UNEXPLORED. He did a bit of sleight of hand, enjoying the wonderment that showed in his daughter's eyes, and produced a small flower. He held it under her nose, letting the scent fill her nostrils.

"It smells so lovely," his daughter said. "What is it?"

I have told one *and* only *one person the secret, and I hope you will remember the scent of* jasmine, *for that person is* you.

Lord Croft gazed lovingly at his daughter as she held the flower out toward him. "Jasmine," he said.

"Jasmine?" she repeated.

"And along the Khmer Trail it only grows on a thirty-mile stretch in a place that no human has seen for a thousand years."

"Jasmine," Lara said, obviously enjoying her newfound wisdom, "a thousand years."

Unable to restrain himself, Lord Croft reached down and picked his daughter up tenderly. He hugged her close, not bearing the thought of the letter he was writing and how, someday, they must be parted. "Angel," he said quietly.

I know you will be there. I wish you luck, and love.

ELEVEN

Croft Manor, England

Lara, dressed for action now, stood at the Library desk and gazed at the letter. She reread the last line at the bottom of the page. " 'What is now proved was once only imagin'd.' " Then she refolded the letter with the notes and carefully returned them to the Blake book.

"Are you ready?" Hillary asked.

"As I'll ever be." Lara looked up at Hillary and Bryce standing at the desk before her. She put the Blake book into her backpack.

"How are you going to get to Cambodia in fifteen hours?" Bryce asked.

Lara stood and pulled the backpack over one shoulder. "I'll be calling in a favor. It's a secret. And I'd have to kill you if I told you."

Nearly twenty-four hours later, Lara plummeted from the belly of a C130 United States Army transport craft. She popped her parachute open, then settled into the drop, following her Land Rover toward the jungle waiting below.

She glanced up, watching the C130 bank and fly away. Over the years, her expertise had been requested and used by several government agencies around the world. Many of them still owed her favors.

The Land Rover touched down first, landing with a harsh bounce despite the carefully rigged parachute. The nylon draped over the surrounding trees and brush. After Lara landed, she quickly cut the parachutes free, rolled them up, and buried them.

She climbed to the top of a brush-strewn hillock and stayed low. The drop had been a good one, bringing her in very close to her target destination. And the way she'd drifted in had kept her from view of the people she knew were below. She fished a pair of high-power, mini binoculars from her backpack and scanned the jungle ahead and below.

Hundreds of Asian laborers worked the massive excavation site. A path had already been cleared to the opening of a buried tomb. A giant stone block with a frieze of a woman was set into the archway, filling the entrance. The laborers hauled on ropes tied to bolts sunk deep into the stone, struggling to pull the block from the entrance.

Above the frieze of the woman, three giant stone heads stared down serenely. One of them stared straight over the entrance while the other two looked to the left and the right.

Lara moved the binocs along, surveying the operation till she found someone she recognized. Manfred Powell stood by another Land Rover, holding an astrolabe in one hand while he surveyed the sky. The clock that had been stolen from the Tech Room sat on the vehicle's hood beside him.

"Mr. Powell," Lara mused to herself, smiling coldly. "How *un*surprising."

Powell turned to show the astrolabe readings to another man.

Lara recognized that man as well. "And Alex West. You greedy, greedy boy. No scruples."

"Did you say Alex West?" Bryce's voice crackled into her everpresent head set.

"Just hired by the bad guys," Lara admitted. *"Bryce."*

"What?"

Lara smiled. "Stow it. Haven't you got work to do?"

"Yes, Your Majesty."

Lara watched Alex West for a moment longer. "Gotcha," she said. The workers just about had the front door of the tomb open. Shifting the binocs skyward, she observed the flash of Aurora barely seen among the clouds. The alignment was almost upon them.

"Okay. Front door's out." Lara retreated to the Land Rover, stripping out of her flying suit as she went. She wore shorts and a tank top beneath. Reaching into the back of the Land Rover, she pulled on her twin .45s and her backpack.

She slid behind the Land Rover's wheel and keyed the ignition. She released the clutch and aimed the all-terrain vehicle through the jungle, knocking down brush and small trees in her haste.

Once Lara located the narrow trail, she stayed with it. There was barely room on either side for the Land Rover to pass.

Abruptly, the trail dead-ended into the hill in a bowl-shaped depression in front of the crumbling ruins. She paused for a moment to study the map drawn by her father. Comparing it with the ruin's layout she noticed that she was in the right place and folded it into the pages of the Blake book.

Sitting in the Land Rover, Lara gazed at the mess made by tree roots that had split and shattered the stone for thousands of years. Still, she could see no way in.

Lara clambered out of the truck and walked toward the ruins. Movement in her peripheral vision drew her attention. Lara turned quickly enough to spot a small peasant girl in a bright saffron dress playing among the trees. The little girl looked like she might have been seven years old, her hair dark and long. Then the girl stopped, diving deeper into the jungle.

"Hey," Lara called as she followed. In the next clearing, Lara paused. The little girl had vanished.

A giggle sounded behind Lara.

Lara whipped around, getting just a glimpse of the saffron dress before the girl disappeared behind a winding tree root. Lara took up immediate pursuit, weaving skillfully through the thrusting tree roots. But when she got to the other side of the large tree, the girl was nowhere to be seen.

A scrambling noise sounded behind Lara. When she turned, she saw the little girl on the other side of the ruin. The girl stood still, smiling, then her features suddenly seemed decades old, making her look ancient.

Lara moved, trying to get a better view of the girl, but when she looked again, the little girl was gone.

Her giggle sounded right behind Lara. Spinning, Lara confronted the girl, who stood at the Land Rover's side. Slowly, Lara approached her.

The little girl waited this time, still smiling. She clutched a spray of jasmine blooms. She spoke in Cambodian. "Those digging men—they are fools. The God-Who-Sees-All will swallow them alive."

"Why?" Lara asked.

"Didn't you see? They tore his lover away from him."

Lara considered that, remembering the large stone frieze of the woman the workers had hauled away from the entrance. "Is there another way?"

The little girl nodded, and for an instant her features looked incredibly old again. "Approach him with a steady hand and a clear eye, and he will let you into his heart." Abruptly, she looked young again. "But he may not let you out."

Lara grinned at her, enjoying the riddles.

The little girl pointed behind Lara.

When Lara turned, she saw three jasmine flowers growing in the gnarled tree roots and broken stone that hadn't been there a moment ago. Curious, she turned back to talk to the little girl again, only to find her gone.

Slowly, Lara walked over to the three flowers. She knelt beside them, surveyed them carefully, then easily picked the first one. The second one came easily as well, but the third jasmine had an exceptionally long root. Tugging harder, she felt the root snap, then the ground opened up.

The hole was small at first, but it continued drinking down the earth. In seconds, the tangled root systems of the trees lay exposed, and below them was a cave.

Lara grabbed the roots and lowered herself into the earth.

TWELVE

The Tomb of the Dancing Light, Cambodia

Lara stood on a balcony at the other end of the tunnel that had led her into the tomb proper. The tunnel she had followed had taken her to a large gallery that hung to the sides of the main tomb high above the cavern floor. She literally had a ringside seat for the action.

She switched off her flashlight and took in the surroundings as Powell's group came into view. Their flashlights cut swaths through the darkness. Then one of them grazed a large dais ahead. An excited murmur passed through the group as all their flashlights converged on the huge six-armed statue sitting near the dais. The statue held six huge swords. An army of monkey-faced soldier statues stood guard in front of the dais.

Powell, Alex, Pimms, and the security team moved in to surround the dais. The Cambodian work group hung back, obviously afraid of what might happen.

Alex walked up to the lead monkey-faced soldier and tapped it on the forehead.

Pimms came slowly up behind Alex, his attention moving swiftly back and forth between the monkey-faced soldiers and the big statue by the dais. "What the . . . heck . . . are those?"

Alex turned to Pimms and Lara noticed that her rival kept his face absolutely neutral. "Monkeys," Alex said.

"Of course," Pimms said. "Very effective."

Alex waited a moment. "Pimms."

"Yes?"

"Do you think you could find your way back to the surface?"

"Well, ah, we marked the way, with those little things, blue flare thingies, so . . . probably."

"Go back to the surface," Alex suggested quietly.

"Well . . . I don't think I can, just yet." Pimms frowned. "I mean, Mr. Powell—"

Alex put a hand on Pimms's shoulder. "Pimms. Buddy. Seriously consider returning to the surface. Now."

"Mr. West!" Powell called out. *"Tempus fugit."*

Lara looked at her watch, then peered over the gallery and agreed with Powell. "Time flies."

Powell took the clock from a pack and held it, studying it. From her position, Lara could see the glowing dials. The three planets had almost aligned.

"We have only minutes left," Powell said, excitement ringing in his voice. "Remember, what we are looking for is hidden not only in space, but also in time." He compared the clock with a high-tech silver chronograph in his other hand.

Pimms joined Powell, skirting around the troops of stone monkey-soldiers. "What do we do now?" Pimms asked.

"The clock is the key," Powell said. "You'll see." He aimed his flashlight at the dais, illuminating the eye socket at the far end.

Lara gathered herself, staying low as she ran around the balcony. Now that the flashlights lighted the tomb, she saw that the balcony was actually a gallery that ran around the whole tomb high above the main floor. Pillars supported the gallery, and those pillars were inscribed with ancient symbols.

As the light in the tomb grew, it revealed the huge statue of the six-armed swordsman sitting across the dais behind the glowing dome. A huge urn of water sat in his lap, bubbling slightly. Roots dripped into the urn from the gnarled mesh of tree roots above.

Alex led the group up onto the dais. He grinned confidently as he played his sword over the gigantic six-armed statue. He waved to the workers. "Okay, guys, let's strip this baby down!"

The workers placed more chemflares on the ground and popped them. The wavering dome reacted at once, leaping at the light. Beams shot out, lighting up the pillars and the runes burned black into them.

Powell held his flashlight over one of the runes. "We are . . . led . . . to believe . . ."

Alex and his men started to pull the swords from the fists of the six-armed swordsman statue. Metal rasped against stone.

Lara moved around the gallery, focusing on the same pillar as Powell, reading it. At first she couldn't make sense of the runes the Illuminati lawyer was reading. Everything looked backward from what she'd expected. Acting on a hunch, Lara drew her knife and turned it so it reflected the runes she was trying to read. Now they made sense; the runes had been written in mirror-writing. "We are led . . . to believe a lie . . ."

". . . a lie," Powell continued, "when we see not through . . ."

". . . the Eye," Lara read.

Under Alex's direction, the workers removed the swords and brought them over to the dais where Powell stood. Alex played his flashlight beam over the six slots carved around the edge. He instructed the workers to sheathe the swords into the slots. The swords grated loudly as they slid deeply into the stone.

"When we see not through the Eye . . ." Powell went on as the swords surrounded him.

"Through the Eye," Lara repeated thoughtfully. She looked into the blade again and her mind raced. "Mirror. Reflection. Reverse." She paused, putting it together. "We are led to believe a *lie.*" She turned around, knowing that Powell had missed an important fact. She stared into the darkness until she found the *second* eye on the wall behind her. The eye Powell was concentrating on was an illusion, and no doubt a trap.

"Forty-five," Alex counted down, watching the silver chronograph as Powell centered the ancient clock over the false eye on the dais, "forty-four, forty-three . . ."

"The timing must be *exact,*" Powell warned.

"Forty-one," Alex said, "no joke, forty-nine . . ."

"But childish," Powell said, irritated.

Alex continued counting.

Unable to wait any longer, Lara stepped to the edge of the gallery and yelled down. "Mr. Powell!"

Powell, Alex, Pimms, the soldiers, and workers all turned immediately, searching for her.

"You're making a big mistake," Lara warned.

Two Illuminati soldiers raised their rifles and opened fire. *Blamblamblamblam!*

Lara ducked away and the bullets didn't even come close.

"Cease fire!" Powell roared. *"Hold your fire!"* After the men stopped shooting, the Illuminati lawyer looked at Alex. "Keep counting."

"Thirty-four," Alex said, "thirty-three . . ."

Lara stepped back into view on the gallery. "Alex West."

"Thirty-one," Alex said, "—Hey Lara—"

"Tourist visa?" Lara asked.

"Twenty-nine," Alex continued, shrugging. "Nah, I'm working. Twenty-seven . . ."

"Lady Croft," Powell cut in. "Is there some *good* reason why I just saved your life? Please explain."

Lara turned to Powell and made her voice forceful. "That's not the true eye."

"This is the eye," Powell argued.

"And I know where the true eye is," Lara said.

"This *is* the true eye."

"It really *isn't,* you know. It's actually a mirror image." Lara knew she had the attention of everyone in the tomb. Alex, Pimms, and the men below kept shifting their attention back and forth between them.

"Miss Croft," Powell said. "I believe you are trying to cheat me out of my little ray of sunshine."

" 'A fool sees not the same tree that a wise man sees,' " Lara quoted.

"What?" Powell didn't seem so sure now.

"Why would I try to cheat you out of anything now? I need you to *get* the piece so I can *steal* it from you later."

"You're bluffing." Powell turned to one of the soldiers standing nearby. "Julius! Make a mental note: Kill Miss Croft if she attempts any such thing."

The man nodded. "Mr. Powell, sir!"

"Sixteen," Alex counted in sing-song cadence, "fifteen . . ."

"Well," Lara said, "we can do it my way, or we can all come back in time for the next alignment, and you're welcome to try and kill me then." She glanced at the clock and saw the three planets approaching alignment. "In another *five thousand years.*"

"Eleven," Alex counted, "ten . . ."

Powell made his decision quickly, throwing the clock high into the air.

Lara caught the clock and quickly slammed it home into the eye on the wall behind her. The swords on the dais sank and rumbling echoed briefly throughout the tomb. A stone panel slid away in the wall near Powell. A lever rose up beside the man.

"Shoot her!" Powell commanded his men.

Lara ducked back into the shadows of the gallery, taking cover behind one of the pillars. Immediately, the security team opened fire. Bullets filled the air, knocking hunks of stone from the railing. Then she noticed the tree trunk suspended at gallery level only a few feet away.

The tree trunk hung suspended by chains and pulleys, secured by a metal eyehook at the end. A pin joined it to the metal eyehook attached to the gallery.

Twisting, Lara gazed over the chipped railing from behind a pillar where she'd taken cover when the initial gunfire died away. Below, Powell grabbed the lever and heaved. The chain tightened and yanked the pin from the two eyehooks. Freed now, the huge tree trunk fell, following the guide ropes toward the urn the statue held.

"Now," Lara said, "is *really* not a good time." She dashed from behind the pillar and vaulted over the gallery railing as the tree trunk shot by. Her boots thudded against the tree trunk high above the tomb. Bullets hammered the tree trunk, causing it to vibrate beneath her.

She drew her knife and ran toward the front of the tree trunk. Seizing the rope that supported the front end of the huge log, she severed it with one stroke.

The front of the tree trunk collapsed, falling down. Lara scrambled back along its length, holding tight to the support ropes. By the time the tree trunk hung straight down, she'd gained the other end of it, riding it down as it swept forward, crashing through Powell's security teams.

Powell brought a rifle up to his shoulder and aimed at the urn. *Blamblamblam!* The urn sprang leaks, pouring the water out, revealing cubes of yellow metal.

Lara recognized the metal. "It's *phosphorus!*"

"Phosphorus?" Bryce repeated over the headset. "Where? You know if air hits it—"

The resulting explosion of light caused by the air hitting the phosphorus and setting it afire washed over onto the silvery-blue dome of the tomb. The dome cracked, then exploded into a column of liquid silver that bounced a kaleidoscope of rippling patterns all over the tomb's interior.

THIRTEEN

The Tomb of the Dancing Light, Cambodia

The Tomb of the Dancing Light, Lara mused as she watched the spectacular light show. *Definitely aptly named.* As the light show progressed, though, there was no sign of the Triangle piece.

"All very, er, lovely," Pimms said nervously, "but where's the piece of the Triangle?"

"Remember, Pimms, it's not just hidden in space, but also in time."

Lara studied the column of silvery-blue liquid squirting up from the dais. "Bryce," she called, "how long till the alignment?"

"Right," Bryce replied, *"now!"*

With a surge of strength, Lara leaped from the top of

the tree trunk, flipping toward the dais. A flicker took shape at the top of the silvery-blue liquid column, then became the Triangle piece.

Powell reached for the piece, but Lara snapped a hand out and grabbed it only inches from the man's fingers. The silvery-blue column collapsed, splashing across the dais and running into rivulets carved into the tomb's floor.

Lara landed in a crouch on the other side of the dais from Powell. With her free hand, she drew one of her .45s and trained it on the man. In the next heartbeat, the weapons of the security team lit her up with laser sights.

"Miss Croft," Powell said pleasantly. "It seems I underestimated you." He smiled. "I promise, it won't happen again."

Lara peered at him above her pistol sights. "I'm going all warm and fuzzy inside."

Powell nodded at the tree trunk. "That was very impressive. I think we could use someone of your abilities—"

"No one uses me, Mr. Powell."

"You don't seem to have many other options at the moment." Powell spread his hands and nodded at his men. They pointed their weapons at her. "Just what do you think you're going to do now?"

"I'm going to walk out of here," Lara stated calmly. "And I'd advise you to do the same."

"Why, precisely, would I do that?"

"It's the only hope you have of getting out alive."

Behind Powell, Alex glanced up at the ceiling, his attention drawn to the drops of silvery-blue liquid that had run up the walls and were now dropping down onto the heads of the stone, monkey-faced soldiers.

"Powell," Alex said, "I think she might be right."

"Don't be," Powell turned around to face Alex and came face-to-face with one of the stone soldiers that had walked up behind him, "ridiculous—"

Lara watched the shadows shift as more of the stone soldiers became animated and stepped up onto the dais. There were still dozens coming. She tucked the Triangle piece into her belt and grabbed for her other pistol.

The lead soldier drew his sword. Immediately, the other soldiers drew their weapons and attacked.

Lara jumped sideways from the dais, firing the whole time, slamming bullets into the stone soldiers that tore them to pieces. Powell's guards quickly circled him and started blasting the soldiers with their AK-47s.

Alex fired, consistently scoring against the soldiers coming for him.

Blasting free of the cordon the stone soldiers had tried to erect around her, Lara aimed her steps at the tomb's entrance up the steep hill.

"Stop her!" Powell roared. "She has the piece!"

A sudden, horrible grinding noise filled the chamber, sounding even louder than the crashing gunfire. Risking a glimpse over her shoulder, Lara saw the huge, six-armed swordsman stand up and draw the six blades from the stone dais.

She felt the vibrations of its weight through the earth as it came after her. "What?" she said in disbelief. She raised her .45s and started firing, knocking hunks from the stone giant.

The swords danced in the six-armed swordsman's hands, weaving a deadly steel net.

Lara slapped a button on her backpack strap and a bandolier tree slid from the bottom of her backpack. She reloaded her weapons, backing away. She ducked under a swipe that would have taken her head off. Suddenly she realized the stone giant wasn't after her. It wanted the piece of the Triangle. Lara holstered a pistol and retrieved the piece. "Hey, West. It's all yours." She threw the piece to Alex.

Alex caught the Triangle piece. "Croft, what the—"

Immediately, the six-armed giant turned on its heels and focused on Alex.

Alex cursed, then fired rapidly, emptying the AK-47 assault rifle he'd picked up. Lara fired rapidly, adding her firepower to his. The bullets gouged deep craters in the immense stone body and even ripped one of the arms off, but the stone creature didn't halt.

Ducking behind a pillar, Alex reloaded. The stone giant slammed into the pillar so hard it cracked. The tomb groaned with the strain. Alex glanced around, caught Lara's eye, and threw the Triangle piece back at her. "No, really, you keep it."

Lara caught the Triangle piece, circling quickly to put the dais between the stone giant and herself.

Powell and Pimms scrambled for cover, trailed by the few remaining security men. The statue leaped toward Lara, who fired quickly. The statue was beginning to take on the appearance of a piece of Swiss cheese due to the barrage of gunfire.

When it landed in front of Lara, the statue raised an arm over its head, intending to bring the sword down through her skull. She took deliberate aim and squeezed the trigger, blasting the statue's arm off at the elbow. Even as the arm dropped to the ground, the statue kept coming at her, following her retreat up the inclined wall.

Lara took aim at another arm and squeezed the trigger, then discovered both the .45s were empty. She holstered them, getting a glimpse of Alex streaking through the confusion toward her. In the next moment, the statue charged straight for Lara, trying to overpower her. Reacting quickly, Lara dropped to the ground and slid down the wall. When she drew even, she kicked the statue in the crotch, breaking free a huge stone mass.

"Man," Alex winced. "That was *cold.*"

Off-balance, the statue staggered, slamming a shoulder into one of the pillars supporting the gallery above. Stone cracked, and this time it wasn't just the statue. Lara pushed up from the ground just as the gallery crumbled, becoming tons of rock that poured down into the tomb.

The other stone soldiers kept closing in on Powell and his group, obviously intending to kill anyone left in the tomb.

Lara ran toward the tomb entrance, struggling up the incline. A group of the stone soldiers stepped in front of her to block the way. Without breaking stride, she vaulted to the shoulders of the first stone opponent, then continued running, using their heads as stepping-stones. She leaped from the last one and caught herself on her hands and feet.

She glanced over her shoulder and saw Powell and Pimms mired in the stone soldiers. The AK-47s kept blasting, but for every stone warrior that went to pieces, another took its place. Lara continued to run up the tunnel from the tomb. With a final leap, she cleared the deadly horde.

Lara sprinted toward the chamber door, passing by the flickering chemflares and straight into the sunlight in the tunnel's mouth beneath the three heads.

The security team Powell had left posted at the entrance reacted too slowly. She was past them, legs churning against the ground, even as their startled shouts rang out around her. Bullets followed immediately afterward, thudding into the trees and dense undergrowth.

Still on the move, she draped the com-link phone back over her ear and keyed up. "Bryce! Bryce! Wake up!"

"Ah, hello, Brycey can't come to the phone at the moment," Bryce said in his best telephone answering machine voice, "but if you leave a message, he'll get back to you as soon as possible. *Beeeeep.*"

Despite the situation, Lara smiled. "Very funny. Ho ho ho." A new welter of gunfire drove Lara to cover.

"Are you okay?" Bryce asked.

"I'm *running.*" Lara used her gloved hands to knock aside trees and brush, aware of the pursuit behind her. The land was crooked, uncertain and treacherous. "East from the tomb. Any thoughts?" Bryce had maps of the area.

"Ah, where are we? Ah . . ." Bryce said.

Blamblamblamblamblam! The top of a young sapling, sheared from the trunk by a stream of bullets, toppled in front of Lara. She vaulted it at the last moment, barely sailing clear of it.

"There's a river!" Hillary shouted over the headset connection.

"There's a river!" Bryce shouted at almost the same time. "Ah, northeast—no . . . hold on, ah, hold on . . ."

"You're putting me on hold?" Lara asked in disbelief. Then she heard the rushing roar of the nearby river. She turned off the com-link phone and stored it in a pouch on her belt. Then she redoubled her efforts, crashing through the jungle growth.

A moment later, she spotted the sparking lights of the river ahead through the trees and underbrush. She smashed through a final barrier of trees and was surprised to discover that she was in a clearing. Nothing stood between her and the river.

"I'll shoot!" a familiar voice warned.

Lara stopped. She heard Alex in the jungle behind her. She gazed at the riverbank, seeing now that it was high above the river.

"Lara," Alex said, "give it up. The other guys will kill you."

Lara didn't turn around. "Well, you know, Alex, I don't know about Tomb Raider, but maybe you could find work in a related field." She tightened the backpack straps, getting ready. "Gravedigger, perhaps."

She threw herself forward in an all-out run, halfway expecting Alex to fire because she could never be certain which side he was on. Then she was at the edge, flinging herself into the long dive.

She heard Alex curse above her and shout, "Now I'm in trouble," then the river accepted her into its embrace, closing over her and pulling her deep.

FOURTEEN

Cambodia

Lara drifted on the river for hours, clutching a large jasmine branch that she'd found when she'd surfaced. She had the Triangle piece, so the threat—for now—seemed distant. She was just trying to plan her next move when she spotted the boats in the water over by the bank.

Lara let go of the branch and turned over in the water to take a better look. The people in the boats washed their clothes in the river, gossiped, and bartered. A group of robed monks sat to one side on the riverbank, deep in meditation. High above the river on the hill overlooking the area stood an ancient temple.

The evening sun streaked gold across the river. Lara swam toward the monks, standing in the water when it was shallow enough. Children running excitedly along the bank laughed and pointed at her.

A young monk, no more than a teenager, opened his eyes and regarded Lara as she stepped from the river.

Drenched and soaking, Lara smiled. She spoke in Khmer. "My phone is wet. Do you know where I can make an international call?"

The young monk smiled broadly, then—surprisingly— chuckled. "Come," he said, rising to his feet. Then he turned and led her up the hill to the temple.

Dressed in a yellow robe and standing on the tallest balcony of the temple nearly an hour later, Lara felt much warmer and relaxed.

It wasn't until she'd gotten cleaned up that she realized there was blood dripping from her shoulder.

An elderly monk adjusted a satellite dish to her left, aiming it at the sky. When he had it properly aligned, he nodded at Lara.

Lara punched her home number into the sat-phone's keypad and listened to the ring.

Bryce picked up at once. "Hello?"

"Bryce," Lara said, "it's me. I'm okay."

A sigh of relief sounded along the phone line. "Did you get the clock?"

"No. But I got the first piece."

"Be-oot-iful. Smashing."

Lara grinned. "Yep. So I think I'm level pegging with Mr. Powell. I feel good."

"Won't he just want to kill you now?"

"Nuh-uh," Lara reasoned. "Piece of the Triangle first, kill me later. And that's going to be his big mistake."

"Killing you?"

"No, silly. I won't ever let him kill me. His problem is that he *needs* the piece I have." Her bleeding shoulder stained her borrowed yellow robe. "Until then, I'm his new best friend." The phone beeped, a second call was coming in. "Got to go. Call you later." She clicked over, answering the second call. "Lara in Cambodia."

"Lady Croft," Powell said smoothly. "I've been scanning all London calls, and there you are. How are you?"

"Alive."

"And kicking, I hope."

"And yourself?"

"Superlative."

"Okay. Bye, then." Lara disconnected. The phone rang again almost immediately, and she had no problems guessing who it was. "Get to the point."

"Of course," Powell said. "I digress. You have my half of the Triangle."

"You have my father's clock."

"Listen, my dear, without each other we are quite useless at this point."

"And we are living, as they say, 'in interesting times.'"

"So, my dear, we should reevaluate our positions. Like it or not, you and I are in business together. We should have a business meeting. We should meet."

"You mean you would like another opportunity to try to kill me."

"Oh," Powell said, "that's harsh." He paused. "But, perhaps. Wait and see. Come to Venice. Via Doloroso."

Lara made her voice hard. "You have ten seconds to tell me all you know about my father's death. Because I'm sure you know *something.*" She disconnected again, then dialed Bryce. "Okay, I'm back."

"But he still has the clock," Bryce pointed out. "He can find the second half. In . . . ah, sixty-six hours, fifty-three minutes. And we have no idea where that might be. Not without the clock."

"Oh, he's going to *tell* me where the second half is. Trust me."

"He will?" Bryce didn't sound at all convinced.

"Well, unless he's got my half and killed me by then, *which he will not.*" Lara disconnected again, then handed the phone to the monk manning the satellite dish. "Thank you."

"Phone drive me crazy," the monk replied in English. "Tiny voices."

Lara smiled. "Necessary evil."

He grinned up at her. "You think? Really?"

Lara shook her head.

A few minutes later, Lara sat in a lotus position in a room filled with hundreds of lighted candles.

The elderly monk who'd let her borrow the sat-phone walked into the room carrying a cup of green tea. He placed the cup in front of her. "Rest," he advised.

Lara picked up the tea and sipped. "No rest for the wicked."

The young monk who had led her to the monastery and kept her company stood and bowed to Lara, who bowed her head in return. Without a word, he left the room.

The elderly monk dropped slowly into a lotus position opposite her. The glow from the candles made his skin look like burnished copper.

"You got what you came for?" the monk asked. His eyes regarded the backpack.

"Yes," Lara answered.

The old monk sighed. "Too bad. Bad for the world."

"The world is safe now."

"Mmmmm. A little bit *safer*, perhaps."

Lara frowned and started to object, but the monk's features softened.

"Because you will go on," the monk told her. "Your father said that you would never give up. And that you would have to keep your will in check."

"My father? You knew my father?"

But the old monk closed his eyes and said nothing.

Wanting to know more of her father's connection to these people, Lara said, "Excuse me."

The monk remained perfectly still, he even seemed to stop breathing.

Did he just die? Lara reached out to touch his arm.

Then the monk's eyes snapped open. His face seemed changed, and Lara could somehow see her father's face in the old man's. "Soon you will have discovered all my secrets."

"Daddy?" Lara asked in disbelief.

"Secrets not even your mother knew . . ." her father continued.

"Secrets?"

"When she died," her father said, "when you were a baby, I suddenly saw my life through new eyes. Your clear, child's eyes, Lara. And what I saw was . . ." He stopped, the memory painful. "Judge me with your heart, angel."

Lara was uncharacteristically unsettled. "I don't understand."

"You must get the clock back, Lara. And destroy it. Or in five thousand years' time, the descendants of Powell will be able to again find the pieces and re-form the Triangle."

"But—"

"*Destroy the clock*, Lara. Close the door. Don't be tempted by the power. I was, but you must be stronger. *Focus*. Eyes on the prize."

"You were tempted, Daddy?"

" 'One thought fills immensity . . .' "

The teacup Lara had been holding smashed against the stone floor, throwing the dark green liquid in all directions. She also noticed that the floor was suddenly six feet below, and she was levitating above it.

"We will help you," the old monk said, once again seeming to be only the old monk.

"You will help me?" Lara said. "You will?"

"You need a little help. The world is in your hands." The old monk's voice changed, and for a moment he sounded a little like her father again. "*Lara. Angel.*"

"I—I don't know what to say."

The old monk looked at her. "Then finish your tea. The words will come to you, later. Now, drink."

Surprised, Lara glanced down. She was sitting on the floor again, and the teacup—unbroken—rested in her hand. She lifted the cup to her lips and drank.

"It tastes quite bad," the old monk admitted, "but it's good for you." He removed his hand from her shoulder and pulled away the bandage that had been applied earlier.

When Lara looked at her shoulder, she found the wound had healed.

Less than twenty-four hours later, Lara Croft lay on a rooftop across from the Illuminati building on the other side of the Grand Canal in Venice.

She trained her binocs on the building, taking in the gargoyle holding the All-Seeing Eye in its claws. She swept the windows and finally came to the one that showed Powell and Alex having a heated discussion. The clock—her father's clock—sat on the conference table between them.

"Getting grumpy," Lara observed. Working together wasn't an easy thing for the two men, and it showed dramatically in the body language.

Powell thumped the table with a fist, underscoring his words, but Alex only shook his head and started arguing.

Lara smiled, feeling somewhat better about the trip and the risk she was taking. "Remember, boys, there's no *I* in *team.*" Having seen what she needed to, Lara stayed out of sight and made her way back into the building.

Alex West stood in the shower in his hotel room, enjoying the steaming heat from the water cascading down his body. He still felt exhausted, but he knew a lot of that was from the unending arguments he was having with Powell.

A tiny *squeak* caught his attention. He froze. There were many possibilities.

He turned his head sharply, but it was too late. The only evidence of the intruder was seven runes, traced in the beaded sweat on the outside of the shower partition.

Alex reached for the sliding door and tried to yank it

open. But it stuck and it was a struggle to get out. He didn't bother with a towel, dripping as he walked out into the two-room apartment. His gear lay everywhere because he hadn't had time to put it away and because he wasn't going to be staying there long, anyhow.

No one was in the room. *Outside,* he thought, glancing at the door that let out into the hallway. He crossed the room swiftly, paused for a moment to get courage up, and yanked the door open.

"Aaaaaaggggggghhhhhh!" a woman screamed.

Unfortunately, though, it wasn't Lara Croft. It was a maid carrying a pile of towels. She was so startled she threw them into the air and they flew in all directions, littering the hallway.

Alex stepped back into his room and slammed the door shut. At the bathroom door, he got another look at the seven marks on the beaded shower glass. They weren't runes. They were letters. TRAITOR. And only one person Alex knew could have, or would have, written those letters. He shook his head.

When he came back out of the bathroom, Lara was sitting calmly on his bed, smiling. "Lara!" he exclaimed.

"Alex." Lara was completely at ease.

"So you think I'm a greedy unscrupulous sellout who'll do anything for money," Alex stated.

"You said it," Lara replied.

"The money part *is* true, I guess," he admitted with a grin, approaching Lara. "And while we're on the subject, I believe you still have something of mine."

"Not yours," Lara corrected. "You mean *Mr. Powell's* beloved piece of the Triangle."

LARA CROFT,
ADVENTURER.

"THE POWER OF THE TRIANGLE IS REAL, LARA."

"To see a world
in a grain of sand,
and a heaven in a
wild flower . . .
Miss you, Daddy."

"MR. POWELL! YOU'RE MAKING A BIG MISTAKE. THAT'S NOT THE TRUE EYE."

"I know what you want, Lara. Perhaps better than you do yourself."

On her way to

save the world.

"I BET IT'S HIDDEN IN THE SUN," ALEX SAID. "EARTH," COUNTERED LARA. "SUN'S TOO OBVIOUS."

LARA RULES.

"Of course. *Mr. Powell's.*"

"Such loyalty," Lara said, with more than a hint of sarcasm.

Alex shrugged. "Possession is nine-tenths of the law." And with that, he reached under his pillow and pulled out a handgun. Unfortunately for him, Lara was unfazed.

"Oho. Man with a gun," she mocked. "I suppose you intend to frisk me." Lara stood and they were toe to toe, eyes locked on each other.

He knew she probably wouldn't have the piece of the Triangle on her, but he rummaged in her backpack just in case. Nothing. Alex tossed the gun on the bed.

"Find what you're looking for?" asked Lara mockingly.

"Not yet," replied Alex. He turned away from Lara to gather his thoughts for just a second. When he turned back to her again, she was gone.

FIFTEEN

Venice, Italy

Lara stood at the floor-to-ceiling window and gazed out at the Grand Canal as sunset draped Venice in reds and golds. She looked up at the gargoyle above, studying again the All-Seeing Eye clutched in one stone claw.

A door opened behind her and she turned slowly to face the expected arrivals.

"Lady Croft," Powell greeted. "Good evening." Before Pimms could follow him into the conference room, Powell closed the doors in his face, sealing him outside. Without speaking, Powell crossed the room and stopped in front of her.

Lara peered at him, seeing the seal of the All-Seeing Eye on the wall behind him just above his head.

Powell took out a cigar and cut the end off with scissors. "Do you mind if I smoke?"

"Yes," Lara replied.

Powell grinned and struck a match, lighting the cigar. "Your father smoked cigars, I believe."

"He did."

"In the summer, it kills the stench of the canals." Powell shrugged. "Well, *masks* it, somewhat." He puffed contentedly on the cigar.

"You're with the Illuminati," Lara said.

"I beg your pardon?" Powell grinned. "There's no such thing. It's just a bedtime story."

Without warning, Lara plucked a throwing knife from hiding, drew back, and threw it. The knife whizzed only inches above Powell's head and embedded in the All-Seeing Eye seal's pupil. "Sorry, I'm bored, Illuminati."

Powell regarded the knife, then turned back to Lara, nodding slightly. "The People of the Light." He stepped closer to her. "Did you know, Lara, that there are twenty-two civil wars raging around the world at this *moment*? Terrible conflicts. Incalculable grief. Loss. Injustice."

Lara met the man's eyes and didn't back away.

"Twenty-two wars," Powell stated. "Without the People of the Light, there would be at least fifty, maybe sixty. More. The Illuminati work beneath the loom, as it were, to weave a golden thread through life's chaos. A life, as they say, that tends for most people to be nasty, brutish, and—"

"Short," Lara said.

"Yes," Powell agreed. "So short. Insultingly so."

"So you're the good guys?"

"Well, my colleagues like to think so." Powell fell silent for a moment, regarding her. "Have you brought my Triangle? No—of course not. You've hidden it somewhere."

"Yes," Lara said. "Otherwise you'd try to kill me."

"I'm not going to kill you."

"I said you'd *try*."

Powell grinned slightly, then turned away from her. "No. You can keep the Triangle you have, and I will keep your father's clock, and we can be partners."

Deliberately, Lara walked to the head of the conference table. "Who sits *here*?"

Powell didn't look at the chair. "We can be partners and go for the big prize. The Triangle of Light."

Lara patted the chair. "Yes, but *who* sits *here*?"

"It's an incredible dream. An *awesome* power. It could set right so many wrongs."

Lara grinned. "Oh, I don't think *you* sit here, do you?" She spun the chair and easily sat in it. "I think you sit *here*." She turned her hand over to an ordinary chair to her left. "Or here." She indicated the chair to the right. "Or maybe even all the way down there somewhere."

Powell smiled. "Oh, not down there. I sit here. Close to the action. On God's right hand, as it were." He paused. "In fact, I now sit exactly where your father used to sit."

"You're lying."

"Actually, not. In fact, your father mentored me in the Order. It was truly an honor. I loved him."

"I don't believe you. My father was not Illuminati. He would have told me."

"Your daddy kept a great many secrets."

"Not from me," Lara argued.

"Oh, my dear," Powell said with a touch of sadness in his voice. "*Especially* from you." He held her gaze. "I know what you want, Lara. Perhaps better than you do yourself."

"I doubt it."

"You are so like your father—the best I've ever seen."

"And why should I help you? My father never meant for you to have the clock. He hid it from you."

"So it seems," Powell agreed. "He broke his oath. He lied to us. To me." He sighed. "Regrettably. You see, I think the more he came to understand the power of the Triangle, the more it . . . worried him."

"And you?"

"Oh, it fascinated me. You see, it gives the possessor the power of God. Anything you wish is yours—" Powell snapped his fingers, "—in an instant. You can build, destroy—you can move back and forth through time. Undo many things." He paused. "Another life with your father, Lara. A second chance. It will be within my power to give."

"But you don't sit in the big chair."

"Lara," Powell said with deadly intensity. "Help me, and you will get what I know you want."

"How do I know if I were to give you the piece you wouldn't kill me?"

Powell produced a throwing knife in a heartbeat and held it just in front of Lara's eye. "Would it make you feel better, on more familiar ground, if I killed you now?"

Lara grinned. "As I said before, you could try."

"Will you reconsider?"

"I might."

Powell turned suddenly and threw the knife, sinking it into the All-Seeing Eye less than an inch from Lara's knife.

Lara strode up the stairs to Alex West's suite of rooms. She felt angry, and a lot of that anger was directed at Alex.

In the hallway, she kicked the door open and went through.

Alex was playing cards with three local lowlifes. The abrupt intrusion made him jump, and his three poker buddies instinctively pulled their guns.

"Not. Now. Guys," Lara said sternly. She switched to Italian. "I need to speak with Alex. Alone." Her intimidating presence was enough to convince them. Even though they held the guns. The three locals holstered their weapons, grabbed their money, and filed out in an orderly fashion. When they were alone, Lara looked Alex dead in the eye and pointedly asked, "Do you want to be a good guy or a bad guy? Or just a guy?"

Alex looked totally shocked by her attitude.

"You're working for bad, bad people, Alex."

Alex stared at her, trying to judge her mood.

"Your problem," Lara continued calmly, "is: You can't be trusted, and that should *not* be acceptable to you."

"I'm just trying to get by," Alex answered. "Earn a little poker money. Have a little fun."

Lara didn't believe him for a second. "Of course," she said. She then stood and picked up a card from the table. She showed him it was the King of Hearts. "Well, I'll be there, in your face, *one step ahead of you,* every step of the way. This is my business now." She threw the card toward Alex's head. The card spun like a boomerang around Alex's head and returned to her hand. When she flipped the card over, it was now the Joker. She slammed the card onto the table, and crossed to the bed. Reaching under it, Lara retrieved the piece of Triangle she had raided from the Cambodian tomb. Alex's eyes widened and he mentally kicked himself for not realizing that she had stashed it there on her earlier visit. He was bested again. Yet Alex couldn't help but smile at Lara's actions. He turned back to the cards and picked up the Joker. A cold steel shaft was suddenly pressed against his temple. Lara bent down and quietly spoke in Alex's ear. "Just so you know, if you cross me on this one, we may not be able to stay friends."

Walking through the military-edition Chinook helicopter, Powell surveyed all the gear they'd brought aboard for the final leg of the mission. He glared at Pimms. His law clerk had been doting on the Illuminati leader, who'd decided to accompany them.

After a moment of continually being ignored by the leader, Pimms joined Powell and spoke quietly. "I think we're in big trouble."

Powell looked at him, unconcerned. He handed the man a small, ornate box bearing the crest of the Eye. "Hold this, will you?"

"They think we have Lady Croft's piece of the Triangle."

"Yes," Powell agreed. "They think it's in the box you are carrying right now."

Pimms looked at the box. "And is it?"

Powell drew a cigar from inside his jacket. "Why don't you worry about something else? Do you think you are dressed warmly enough? We're going very far north, you know."

Pimms glanced into the box suspiciously. "Oh my God. It's empty. What are we going to do?"

"Guard that box with your *life*." Powell smiled broadly. "You've been entrusted with a huge responsibility."

"And is it still the case that we have no chance of success without that piece?"

Powell put his hand on Pimms's shoulder. "Zero. But don't dwell on it."

"But—"

Powell stepped away from the man, smiling broadly as he saw Lara Croft approaching the helicopter. "*Lady Croft.*"

As if totally unconcerned, Lara strode through the Illuminati guards.

"I knew you would change your mind," Powell told her. He snapped his fingers. After a slight delay, Pimms opened the ornate box.

Lara dropped her piece of the Triangle into the box. "You'd better be ready for this." She closed the box herself, then turned on her heel and walked away.

Powell grinned after her. "Glad to have you aboard, Lara."

Lara stepped from the helicopter and joined Bryce on the tarmac.

Bryce stood in the sunlight wearing full-on Arctic gear and looking like the Michelin Man in boots. "And what am *I* doing here?" He'd accompanied her to Venice, and not been exactly happy to learn they were turning themselves over to the bad guys.

"Saving the universe."

"Even after you just *gave* the bad guy our half of the Triangle?"

"Trust me. I have a plan."

"An insane, reckless kind of plan that you will not be

sharing with me just at this moment?" Bryce sounded almost hopeful.

Lara grinned. "Something like that."

"And we'll save the world and all?"

"Absolutely."

Bryce shrugged. "Okay then."

Alex sat at the other end of the cabin from Lara when the helicopter took off. There was no mistaking that wintry look she gave him. Then she turned away, giving him the cold shoulder as well. He turned his own attention to Powell, Pimms, and the distinguished gentleman who was the Illuminati leader seated in the helicopter's plush executive cabin with him.

"Quite a character, Lady Croft," the Illuminati leader said.

Alex grinned. "Quite."

The distinguished gentleman turned to Powell. "Are we sure she's . . . necessary?"

"Well," Powell said. "One Tomb Raider is good, two: better."

"Oh," Alex corrected quietly, "Lara's the Tomb Raider. Not me."

The Illuminati leader glanced at him. "And you've never before pooled your resources?"

"Ah, no," Alex said. "Well, not like this."

Seated inside the Chinook helicopter, Lara gazed at the turbulent blue-gray skies that lay all around them. Five black-clad security guards sat on the other side of the helicopter's cargo area from Bryce and her. All of them carried

Uzis. Powell evidently wasn't in the mood for taking chances with her.

"Oh-oh," Bryce moaned, "my bum's gone to sleep again. All down the left cheek."

"Suck it up, soldier," Lara told him.

"Are we on the team here?" Bryce asked. "Or have we been kidnapped?"

"Neither," Lara answered calmly.

"Neither?" Bryce repeated in disbelief.

One of the black-clad soldiers nodded at her almost imperceptibly.

Lara glanced at Bryce, noticing the anxious look on his face. "Listen, it's going to be fine."

"It is?" he asked hopefully.

"It is."

"Oh, yes. The *plan*."

Lara shifted her attention back to the security leader as she took out one of her pistols. She racked the slide and let it snap back into place. The noise sounded loud in the helicopter.

Once the Chinooks landed at their destination deep within Siberia, Powell stepped out onto the broken, snow-covered terrain. He wore an Arctic suit but still felt the harsh chill of the wind hammering against him, prying for weak spots.

He glanced at the other helicopter, making sure the assault team there had Lara Croft well-guarded. Despite her desire to see her father again, and the fact that he was the only one who could make that happen, Powell didn't trust her.

He gazed around the land, trying to imagine the impact of the meteor slamming into the earth over five thousand years ago. The huge crater it had made lay within the scraggly tree line higher up the incline. That was their true destination.

The Illuminati leader, also dressed in Arctic gear, stepped up beside Powell, reminding him that his success was necessary to his continued survival. "How much longer?"

Powell took out the clock and consulted the second glowing dial. The three planets there were almost in alignment. "A few hours. But we have to take the last hour overland." He nodded at the crater. "The helicopters will not fly within two miles of the tomb's core."

"We can't fly?" Pimms asked.

"Electromagnetic effects. It's a dead zone."

"So how much longer in total?" the Illuminati leader asked.

"Three hours," Powell responded.

"Precisely?" the Illuminati leader pressed.

Trying to keep the irritation from his voice, Powell said, "Three hours and three minutes. And twenty-five seconds, as of one second ago, when I began to say the word *twenty.*"

Then Alex West spoke up. "Hey, should we synchronize our watches?" No one offered to do so. "Okay."

Without another word, Powell turned from the Illuminati leader and walked toward the group of waiting Inuit nomads who had come down out of the hills to watch the helicopters land.

✣   ✣   ✣

Lara passed down the line of sled huskies being offered in exchange for Powell's gold. She had an eye for the animals, knowing which would stick when the going got tough, and which would give up.

Alex walked past her, making his selection of animals quickly. Lara couldn't help but laugh at one of Alex's choices. The animal was way past its prime years.

Hearing her, Alex turned and glared, then rejected the dog. The Inuit nomad who had offered the animal chuckled a little to himself as he led the husky away.

Rumbling filled the air and four large amphibious vehicles rolled into the gathering. A Siberian army captain jumped down from the first vehicle and walked over to Powell.

Lara was close enough to hear the conversation.

"Sir," the Siberian captain greeted.

"I asked for five vehicles."

"We lost one on the way. It was a very hazardous journey. We lost two men."

"Next time," Powell said, "set out earlier, prepare better, try harder. Now help us load."

As Lara passed through the lines of sled dogs, a small girl joined her.

The little girl spoke in Pidgin Russian. "Are you going out across the ice-lake?"

"Yes," Lara answered, speaking in her language.

"To the crater?"

"Yes, the meteor crater."

"There are devils out there. The Tomb of Ten Thousand Shadows."

"That's right."

"Time is broken there," the little girl warned. "You will lose your mind. Don't go."

"I have to."

"You're risking everything to see him again."

A cold chill that had nothing to do with the wind or the temperature thrilled through Lara. "To see who?"

"Your father."

At first, Lara thought she hadn't heard right.

"One thought," the little girl said, "fills immensity."

Lara's breath caught in her throat for a moment. "Where did you hear that? Who told that to you?"

A shrill whistle captured Lara's attention for a moment. She glanced back at the old nomad rounding up the dogs. When she looked back, the little girl was gone.

Only her words of warning lingered—and one small jasmine flower that shouldn't have been there at all.

Lara picked up the flower and breathed in the heady scent. She shifted her attention to the uphill grade leading to the ancient meteor crater. There was no way she couldn't go.

Lara sat behind the wheel of her amphibious vehicle and watched the convoy spread out across the harsh terrain of the ice-lake.

Powell and Pimms rode in the lead black Humvee, followed by the Illuminati leader and his personal group of bodyguards. ATVs leading the pack dogs rumbled alongside the convoy.

"Oh, come *on*," Bryce protested from the passenger seat. He held his laptop computer across his thighs. The screen had been showing GPS tracking of the area. Now the screen was all distorted.

"Welcome to the dead zone," Lara said.

"Okay. About a hundred yards, I reckon."

"I'm betting fifty," Lara said.

"Eighty," Bryce argued.

Only a moment later, the engines of every vehicle sputtered and died as the electromagnetic activity shut it down. Lara let her vehicle coast downhill for a time.

"Okay," Bryce said, closing the useless laptop. "Fifty."

Slowly, the convoy of vehicles rolled to a stop. "Dead zone," Alex announced. The sled dogs remained sprightly and active, yipping their enthusiasm for whatever hunt they were taking part in.

Lara switched off the ignition, grabbed her backpack from the vehicle's rear deck, and jumped out. "Come on."

"Now?" Bryce whined.

Lara grinned. "Come on, you lazy git. Chop chop."

Grumbling and cursing, Bryce unwillingly climbed from the amphibious vehicle. "It's very cold, you know."

"It's *invigorating*. Come on, Brycey, this is *life!*" Lara replied, taking out her palm-sized telescope.

"This is a large *ice cube*."

Lara studied the harsh terrain through the telescope. She spotted the large black hole in the center of the ice-lake almost at once. "Not for long."

"Okay, what's next?"

Lara grinned. "Nothing but trouble." She collapsed the telescope and went to join the others in sorting out the dog teams for the rest of the journey to the crater.

SIXTEEN

Siberia

Lara leaned into the sled, urging her team on into the teeth of the frigid wind whipping down from the crater. Alex drove his team nearby, making a point of not looking at her. Powell also drove a team, and the Illuminati leader rode as a passenger of a sled driven by one of his personal bodyguards. Bryce drove a team as well, grinning and exulting in his mastery of the dogs while Pimms held on less happily as his passenger.

A few minutes later, they all came to a halt at the crater's edge and peered down. The crater was conical in shape, and at the very eye of it was the cave that led to the underground tomb. The Tomb of Ten Thousand Shadows.

Lara sipped water from her canteen, then gazed up at the sky. The dim outlines of the moon were just starting to skate across the face of the sun. Then she turned her attention back to the sled, stripping off all but the most basic necessities.

Bryce joined her, helping her take equipment and supplies off under her guidance.

Lara caught Bryce's eye. "If Powell comes back up alone," she said quietly, "send in the cavalry."

"And who would that be?" Bryce asked.

"That would be you."

Bryce sobered immediately. "Yikes."

Lara glanced at him. "Did you just say *yikes?*"

Bryce hesitated. "I may have. Good luck."

Lara shook her head and grinned. "It's not luck. It's *timing.*" She stood back on the sled and got the team into motion, leading the way into the crater. The runners slid smoothly, shushing across the frozen snow.

Bryce stood at the top of the crater and watched as Lara disappeared into the cave mouth below. He didn't have a good feeling about it, but at least he was here instead of sitting back in London worrying about her. Being here, he realized, was better. It made the worrying much, much *closer,* was what it did actually, and that was really not much of an improvement.

He took a thick piece of polarized glass from one of the equipment bags and held it up to the sun. The sky was starting to darken now as the eclipse kicked into high gear.

Pimms stood beside him, also peering through a section of the dark glass. "Hmmm," Pimms said. "There are no birds."

"Because there's no life here," Bryce said. The eclipse

covered a quarter of the sun now. Aurora flashes lit up the sky, seeming to charge the air. "According to the ancient Egyptians, after death you have six souls. Your second soul represents energy, power, and light."

The security teams left around the crater's rim stared up into the sky. Most of them seemed nervous.

Bryce didn't blame them. He felt pretty creeped out himself. "The second soul's name is Sekem."

"I wouldn't know," Pimms admitted. "I find things like that a little spooky."

"And you joined the *Illuminati?*" Bryce asked in disbelief.

Pimms didn't reply.

Shaking his head, Bryce looked back at the eclipse in progress. He lowered his voice and made it melodramatic, thinking it wasn't right that he was the only person up there scared to death. Pimms had it coming. "The sixth soul is the Shadow, Khaibit. Khaibit is your memory, and all your pasts. All your deeds, good and bad."

A third of the sun vanished behind the huge moon, and the darkness deepened around them.

Lara glanced around the walls of the tomb in awe. There, stretched in grotesque shapes and hammered into the fused stone, stood shadows of people who had died in one amazing flash of supernova heat, their voices seemingly filling the tomb.

"The original enemies of the People of the Light," Lara said in a soft voice. "Annihilated."

"Whoa," Alex said.

"Death was everywhere."

Powell approached, coming up behind Lara. "The Tomb of Ten Thousand Shadows," he declared. "Come along, children. We've seen the sights." He put his hands on Lara's and Alex's shoulders.

Lara shot Powell a warning look and he removed his hand.

The main chamber of the tomb was only a few moments ahead. The security teams popped chemflares into life, filling the massive chamber with light. More lights aimed overhead revealed the presence of a gigantic metal orrery high above.

It was just like the brass model of the planets back at Croft Manor, but at least fifty times the size and covered in seaweed. Standing several stories tall, the motionless metal shone in the chemflares' light, but it had a luster unlike anything Lara had ever seen.

The Illuminati leader mopped his brow. He was not comfortable here.

Powell moved ahead and took control of the situation. "Bring the dogs," he commanded the leader of the team he had brought with him. "Survey the area."

The soldiers spread out immediately and began shining their lights everywhere. Defying the frozen tundra above, the heat in the tomb became unbearable. Lara and Alex stripped away unnecessary clothing as they eyed the orrery.

"I bet it's hidden in the Sun," Alex said.

"Earth," countered Lara. "Sun's too obvious." Lara observed the soldiers' beams bouncing crazily from planet to planet, twisting into unfathomable knots before finally disappearing into the blackness above.

One of the sled dogs walked into an intersection of those bouncing lights and she watched it seem to come apart, then re-form. The dog looked very confused.

"Wow," Alex said.

"Timestorm," Lara said. "Time is broken here."

"No joke."

"Try to avoid those areas," Lara instructed. "Or you can wait here. Watch my stuff."

Alex ignored her and uncoiled a length of rope. "My fifty bucks says the piece is inside the Sun."

Lara shook her head. "Incorrigible!"

"In-what-able?" Alex asked.

Lara shot him a look and the race was on. The two of them quickly cast rope lines for Saturn's rings, and began to climb. Powell had his men train their weapons on the pair so they wouldn't even think of double-crossing him. And he had three others launch their own lines and climb in pursuit.

"Well," Alex said, as they reached their goal, "that was pretty easy." But he was breathing a little hard.

Lara rolled her eyes and held out a hand. "Give me the clock, please."

Alex dug the clock from his pack as they hung from the rope lines. The clock's second dial glowed diamond-bright. "It's gonna be inside the Sun. I'm telling you."

"We'll see about that," Lara said, looking around. Powell's men had now each reached a planet as well.

Alex held on to the clock, but his gaze was drawn to the static row of planets ahead. "Anyway, it's a cakewalk. It's a giant Jungle Gym. Where's the challenge?"

There was a rumbling and the orrery suddenly lurched

and began spinning madly. Lara was barely able to hold on to Saturn's rings and watched helplessly as Alex was unceremoniously dumped from Saturn, onto Jupiter. Powell's men weren't as lucky and wound up crushed by the gears below. Alex's hold on Jupiter slipped and he grabbed a planetary arm and held on for dear life. He dropped his flashlight, but the clock was still firmly in his grip.

Sudden gunfire ripped through the tomb.

Lara gazed down and saw Powell holding a smoking Uzi.

"Focus," Powell ordered.

Alex threw himself into a death-defying leap across the orrery and landed on Earth. At the same time, Lara released her hold and flung herself toward Mercury. She flipped effortlessly and landed on the small planet near the Sun. She saw Alex searching Earth for a place to put the clock.

"Hey! What are you doing?" Lara demanded.

"You said it was in the Earth! *I won.*"

Lara shook her head as their separate orbits took them apart. "Give me the clock! *You were right!*"

"But—" Alex stared after her, processing what she had said. "Did you just say you were wrong?" he asked smugly.

"I said you were right."

"Lara, forget about the clock. I just wanted to win. And I did. But now we save the world, right?"

"Alex, not now!" Lara said.

"The eclipse will be over in a few minutes, and we're safe for another five thousand years. Yes?"

Lara shot him a look.

"Or no?" Alex asked. "Lara—"

"Trust me!" Lara shouted.

"I don't understand! I'm being a good guy, aren't I?"

"Alex!" Lara shouted. *"Give me the clock!"*

Below, Powell aimed the Uzi at Alex. *"Give her the clock!"*

Shrugging, Alex threw the clock as the orbits came close again. "Okay."

Lara caught the clock in one hand. She looked through the clock's eye at the rings on the Sun. Locating the correct placement, she thrust the clock into its rightful place. The Sun began to glow and vibrate. Lara focused on the phenomenon before her, unaware of anything else in the tomb. Alex called out to her, but with one swift movement, Lara leaped onto the Sun which shattered. When the Sun re-formed, Lara had disappeared, swallowed up in the break in time.

Alex leaped onto the Sun, desperately searching for some way into the resealed giant metal ball.

Then, in the next moment, the Sun opened a flaming hole in its side and spat Lara out in an arc across the orrery. The second piece of the Triangle glinted in her fist. The All-Seeing Eye was clearly embossed on one side.

The orrery finally came to a halt in full alignment.

Lara and Alex climbed back across the planets, then down the ropes. They reached the ground. But the tomb was filling with water. The Illuminati leader, surrounded by his bodyguards, seemed oblivious to the changing physical conditions. His men aimed their weapons at Lara.

She placed the second half of the All-Seeing Eye into the man's hands.

He held the treasure and spoke as if he were in a trance. "We will unite these two parts; the past and the present." The leader then brought the two pieces closer together. "Let us twist all of time into this one moment to fulfill our sacred promise to our ancestors."

The faces of all who surrounded him were tense. Except for Powell's. Even the strange ghostly whispers of those long dead couldn't rattle the man who had long considered this his destiny.

The Illuminati leader continued his incantation. "What is now proved was once only imagined. As a new heaven is begun, eternal hell revives . . . to every man is given the key to the gates of heaven. The same key opens the gates of hell."

Powell exhaled a loud, bored sigh. "Enough of this," he declared. Lara and Alex were powerless to stop what happened next.

Powell's security teams leveled their weapons and opened fire. The bullets kicked into the Illuminati leader and his bodyguards. The Triangle fell from the dead man's hands to the ground.

Bryce was staring up at the near-eclipse, watching the thick shadows move across the ice-lake, when the sounds of gunfire came from the tomb's mouth.

Pimms looked at him.

"Okay," Bryce said in a soft voice. "Here comes the cavalry."

"What?" Pimms asked.

Bryce moved off. "Private joke." But he didn't feel like

laughing. This couldn't have been part of Lara's plan, could it?

Powell strode forward and plucked up the All-Seeing Eye.

Alex felt certain Lara was about to make her move. But she didn't. Powell fit the two halves of the All-Seeing Eye together.

"Got what you wanted?" Lara asked coldly.

The two pieces glowed in Powell's hands, and the bright light fused them together. The glow continued to grow for a moment, then died away. And nothing else happened. Powell looked completely flummoxed, staring at the apparently useless Triangle in his hands.

"Not what you hoped for, Mr. Powell?" Alex asked.

"Oh, Lara," Powell said with amazing calm. "I have a gut instinct about this." He flicked one hand, and a small throwing knife appeared as if by magic.

Alex shifted slightly, but Lara stood her ground in open defiance.

Powell twirled the knife nonchalantly. "After all, you are the daughter of a genius. Let me test my theory." In a flash, he threw the knife and it pierced Alex's heart.

Alex was hurled back from the force of the impact, and landed at the base of the orrery. He slowly sank to the cavern floor that was now covered with several feet of water. *Crack!* The arm of Saturn broke and collapsed onto the stricken Alex. His body was trapped under the planet and his legs pinned down by its rings.

"Alex," Lara cried out as she ploughed through the water between them.

"I'm good," Alex said from his trapped position.

"You're good?"

"You lost the bet. You said Earth and it was the Sun."

"I was wrong," Lara admitted.

The last thing she heard as the water surged over Alex's head was, "You owe me fifty."

SEVENTEEN

The Tomb of Ten Thousand Shadows, Siberia

Stunned, Lara looked down at Alex. His pulse, weak and thready, was fading fast.

"Very touching," Powell commented.

Lara looked up at the man. She never gave up anything this easily. She plunged under the water and found Alex. Her lips found his, and she breathed air into him, then surfaced for more air.

Powell spoke again. "I'm pretty sure you have figured out the answer to the . . ." he waved at the All-Seeing Eye, ". . . *problem.* You have that clever look about you."

Lara ignored Powell, and dove underwater again, bringing air and life to Alex. Each time she resurfaced she faced the persistent presence of Powell.

"You can't keep breathing for him forever, you know. He's bleeding to death anyway."

Lara threw her weight against the orrery arm that pinned Alex in the water. Nothing.

"Now," Powell said. "You could show me how to complete the Triangle and have a chance to change his fate. If you deliver to me the Power of God, I will spare him. *Cogito, ergo est.*"

Lara stared Powell down. Then she returned to Alex to give him another breath of air. Powell waited patiently until she emerged again.

"If I'm wrong," Powell said, *"which I doubt,* you can go home toting a body bag. But if you solve this puzzle for me, I could change that." He paused and lowered his voice. "Your father . . . I could change that."

Lara's control over her anger almost slipped, but she held on to it with an iron will.

"But you must decide soon." Powell glanced at his watch. "There's only about a minute left of the alignment." He pointed at Alex. "And then: *pfffft.*"

Lara jumped up and stood eye to eye with Powell. "You better be ready for this," she warned. She dove underwater one last time to Alex then rose. She walked to one of the security men. "Unhook your laser sight."

The man looked at Powell.

"Do it!" Powell ordered.

Lara took the detached laser sight and swept the red beam around the tomb. The laser continued in a straight path until it hit one of the points beneath the orrery that she had noticed earlier. In a heartbeat, one of the few she was all too aware that Alex had left to him, the reflected red beam twisted into knots and diverted into multiple beams.

Seizing her father's clock, Lara hurled it into the knot. The clock exploded into its separate parts, which froze in midair. At the heart of it all was a tiny, glowing crystal.

Lara ran toward the clock. She leaped high, arm outstretched, reaching for the crystal. Her hand closed around it and there was a translucent flash like a living 3-D X ray. Then she was falling down again, landing and rolling to her feet automatically. Her hand glowed from the tiny crystal it held, while far above her, the outside world was completely dark. The eclipse had reached the total phase.

Lara turned and walked back toward Powell. He held the assembled All-Seeing Eye out toward her. She placed the crystal into the Eye's pupil.

"To see a World in a Grain of Sand," Lara quoted.

Instantly, the pupil started glowing white-hot.

Astonishment widened Powell's eyes.

Drawing back her fist quickly, Lara punched it through the Triangle, through the glowing light it had become, and hit Powell full in the face.

The light spread outward, engulfing Lara and Powell in its glow.

When Lara could see again, she could have sworn she was looking into the Illuminati High Counsel Chambers. There she saw Powell consumed with envy as he watched her father talking with the Illuminati leader. The light was still intensely bright, and when Lara blinked, she found she was standing in front of Croft Manor. "Come on," a young girl called. Then she ran across the driveway, heading for the main door. Lara trailed the little girl through the house, ending up in the Library that she knew so well.

A figure stood against the too-bright window, and he turned at once. Lara knew her father's smile immediately. Then she recognized the little girl as herself, when she was seven, before she'd lost her father. Lord Croft bent down and scooped up his young daughter. Overcome with emotion, Lara closed her eyes. When she opened them she found that it was her present self, not her younger image, embracing her father.

"Lara," Lord Croft whispered. "My Lara."

"Daddy," Lara said, as she fought back tears.

"Yield," her father said. "Give in to the Power of the Light." He leaned forward and whispered in her ear. "Give up. Surrender." He embraced her.

Lara broke free of the embrace and watched as her father's face dissolved into Powell's grinning leer. He pointed a revolver at her forehead.

Closing her eyes, Lara saw another vision. This one was in the Tomb of Ten Thousand Shadows. Powell held the revolver to her father's head this time. Her father stared at him, defiantly.

Powell pulled the trigger and the detonation sounded like a cannon going off inside the cavern.

When Lara opened her eyes again, tears blurring her vision, she saw that they were back in the Library at the manor house. Only this time the Library was on fire.

Powell stood in front of her, his eyes blazing.

On the other side of the Library, a ring of fire trapped Lara's younger self.

"Don't be scared," Lara called to her younger self.

"Oh, I think you should be scared," Powell told the young Lara. "You're going to die."

Lara wheeled to face him, stubborn determination driving her now.

"You died in a fire like this," Powell told her. "You never lived."

"In your *dreams,*" she snarled to Powell.

Abruptly, Powell burst into flames and then was gone. As was the fire that had raged in the Library.

Lara turned and looked into the eyes of her younger self. Young Lara gazed up at her and grinned. Everything was all right now.

Then there was a rustle of movement behind Lara. She turned immediately, hands rising before her defensively. She stood in a moonlit wilderness. Her father's tent was tied down on a high hill. The canvas flaps fluttered in the breeze and lantern light glowed from within.

Lara took one step toward the tent and suddenly discovered herself inside it. Her father stood by his field table and stared at his daughter.

Lara's throat tightened so much it hurt. This *was* her father, not an illusion created by Powell. "Daddy!"

"Lara."

She stepped toward him. "Is this real?" she asked.

"It is a crossing . . . of my past and your present . . . 'to hold infinity.' I must say, you've grown up beautifully."

"Why did you not tell me about the Illuminati?"

Her father sighed and shook his head sorrowfully. "You were only a child."

"But you could have written in your journals. You never mentioned it. Not once."

Her father hesitated. "Lara, precious—I burst to tell you everything. But, in the fierceness of my battles, I strove to tell you only that which would inspire you and keep you safe. I love you so much! You know that!"

Tears filled Lara's eyes. "But I've missed you!"

"And I've missed you!" her father went on. "I know why you've come here. Why you took the Power of the Light. But this must not happen."

"Why? Why can't we use the power—just this once? Why can't you stay?"

"And why can't *you* wear a dress? That's the Eighth Wonder of the world to me! But you can't! Or be caged! Or made to sit and listen to old boring rules? You are *alive* in pursuit—you can't change who you are—and we can't change time."

Lara listened, not wanting to hear.

"Not even your mother knew," Lord Croft went on. "And when she died, when you were a baby, I suddenly saw the Path of the Illuminati through new eyes, as if I were looking through your clear child's eyes, Lara." He paused. "And what I saw was greedy, vengeful, heartless. What drew me in as a young man began to disgust me. Power had eaten away at our souls. We had *become* the Beast."

"But time was stolen from us and that's not fair," Lara said.

"No, it's not fair. But that's how it must remain. The future is yours now, Lara. Destroy the Triangle. You can do it. You're the strongest person I've ever known! The only one with the strength to set or make this right. I'm deeply proud of you!" He looked at her. "I know. I know. But the Power of the Triangle is the power of a *god*. To take that power—*cogito ergo est*—that would be to steal free will from all others. Their lives would simply become figments of a dream *you* were having. And that's not life—that's death." He touched her cheek, stroking her skin, wiping away her tears. "Save Alex, not me."

Tears rolled down Lara's cheeks, but she knew her father was right. "Suddenly I feel so alone!"

"Now you listen to me. You're never alone! I'm with you—always. Just as I've always been. And don't pretend you haven't heard my voice."

Despite the sadness of the moment, Lara had to laugh. She had heard his voice many times.

"So now," Lord Croft said, "Lara, fight on! Be brave! Have *fun!*"

Lara nodded. Her father extended his arm toward her. She stretched out and touched his fingertips with her own. Then she stepped through the tent flap and walked away, looking back over her shoulder at him.

When she reached the end of her walk, Lara was back inside the Tomb of Ten Thousand Shadows. And she was the only thing moving.

Powell and Alex stood only a few feet apart, frozen in place. The throwing knife hung stationary in the air between them. She'd arrived back a minute earlier, just in time to save Alex.

Lara stepped forward and drew her .45s. She aimed at Powell and fired. The bullets passed right through Powell and vanished into the wall on the other side of him without making a sound.

Calming herself, Lara mused, "Okay. Okay. That's not going to work. Have to work with what we've got." She reached for the knife. It glowed with radiant energy and felt like she'd taken hold of red-hot metal. She expected smoke to come from burning flesh. Blood ran down her hand, but her resolve was stronger than the pain. She tried to change the direction of the knife. Powell stood there frozen in time. Yet fully aware. Throwing all her strength into moving the knife, Lara suddenly felt the world tilt. The knife remained static, but the world around it rotated weirdly, as Lara literally made a 180 degree change of fate.

Lara stepped back, staring at Powell. He was now directly in the knife's path. And time once again ticked on.

Almost faster than the eye could follow, the throwing knife flipped through the air and embedded in Powell's shoulder. Surprise, then pain, filled the man's eyes.

Alex dropped back and flinched, thinking the knife was still coming at him. He almost ended up back underwater, but Lara yanked him to safety.

Powell fell backward and the Triangle tumbled from his lax hands. The All-Seeing Eye spun as it fell, then shattered into a billion pieces against the stone floor.

The security team stepped forward at once and leveled their Uzis.

EIGHTEEN

The Tomb of Ten Thousand Shadows, Siberia

Lara and Alex dove for cover as the tomb began to crumble. Water flooded in at an alarming rate. Lara drew his pistols and set herself behind the pile of rock where they'd hidden.

The thunderous roar of the impending collapse filled the tomb. Rocks dropped like hail throughout the cavern.

"Cease fire!" the security team leader yelled above the din. "Exfiltrate! Plan C!"

Immediately, the security men broke off their attack and raced for their sleds.

"What are you doing?" Powell demanded.

Alex peered over Lara's shoulder. "What are *they* doing?"

Lara didn't reply, keeping her attention on the security team and Powell.

"What is Plan C?" Powell demanded.

The team leader turned to Powell, his face cold and emotionless, as if he faced this sort of thing every day. "Our mission is *compromised,* sir. We have failed."

Powell shook his head in disgust. "Oh, thank you, Julius."

"*You* have failed," the security team leader went on. "I must now take care of my men." Another shudder ripped through the cavern, causing the man to stagger slightly, but he kept his footing. "Time's up." He turned and left, heading toward his men.

"Thank you," Powell called after him. "Thank you for nothing."

Lara pulled at Alex's arm, then guided him out around the perimeter of the fleeing security team. The lights flickered, plunging the cavern into split seconds of darkness and uncertain illumination. Everything was coming down; Lara had no doubt about that.

A moment later, she came face-to-face with Bryce and Pimms. Both men had driven sleds down into the cavern instead of fleeing.

Lara locked eyes with Pimms, but she spoke to Bryce. "Well done. Good cavalry." She bent down and took up a discarded Uzi from the ground.

"It was nothing," Bryce said nonchalantly, but he looked around fearfully at the collapsing tomb.

"Nothing at all," Pimms added, trying to act casual as well.

"Mr. Pimms," Lara said pointedly.

Pimms drew himself to his full height and nodded to acknowledge her address of him. "Miss Croft."

Lara pointed the Uzi at Pimms. "You are still one of the bad guys?"

"Absolutely not," Pimms assured her.

"Promise?" Lara asked.

"Promise."

"Cross her heart, and—"

"Hope absolutely to die," Pimms finished. "Absolutely."

Lara tossed the man a wink as she lowered the Uzi. "Good,"

Pimms sighed thankfully.

Alex slapped the man on the shoulder. "Pimms, buddy!" Alex said. "Good call!"

Lara took the lead again, heading for the sleds. A voice called out from behind her, stopping her in her tracks.

"Lara!" It was Powell.

Lara let Alex pass as she glared back at Powell. The man stood behind her and showed no fear at all.

"Good luck," Lara told him coldly. "You're going to need it." She turned and continued following Alex.

"Your father begged for his life," Powell yelled over the grinding rock.

Anger ignited in Lara like a nuclear forge. She stopped, trying to stay on top of it.

"Like a baby," Powell went on.

Cold and deadly calm inside, Lara turned to face her tormentor. "I don't think so."

Powell offered her a nasty smile. "Well, now you'll never know, will you?" He produced her father's pocket watch, twirling it on its long chain.

Even from the distance, Lara saw her mother's picture on the inside lid as the pocket watch spun.

"He seemed particularly concerned that I shouldn't take this . . ." Powell kissed the picture inside the lid. ". . . from his cold, dead body."

Lara started walking toward Powell. She ignored the sudden blast of cracks that shifted another load of rock loose overhead and let it crash around them.

"Lara!" Alex called behind her. "Leave him! No, no, no!"

Lara kept walking, ignoring Alex's pleas.

Alex was determined not to let her play Powell's game. Running alongside her he pleaded, "Don't pull the 'Who Dares Wins' stuff on me now, Lara! Please. We gotta get out of here. This whole place is gonna collapse."

But there was no stopping her now.

Standing on the trail on a rise above Powell, Lara towered over the man. Powell smirked up at her, and more than anything Lara wanted to remove that smirk or punch it through to the back of his head.

"Lara!" Alex continued pleading. "We're gonna be freakin' *pancakes* in about *two minutes!*"

Lara lunged forward to snatch her father's pocket watch from Powell's hand. But in one, swift move, Powell yanked the pocket watch from her grasp, lunged forward and slashed at her with a previously concealed stiletto.

Pain electrified Lara as Powell's blade cut into her leg. Alex reacted instantly, lashing out and kicking Powell in the head.

"Hey!" Alex bellowed. Not exactly the words of a knight in shining armor, but heartfelt nonetheless.

Lara refocused and regained her balance, pushing the

pain from her mind and focusing instead on the anger that filled her. She jumped in between Powell and Alex.

Powell recovered more quickly than should have been possible. Lara guessed that he'd been faking injury, because Powell struck out immediately with another knife, driving it at Lara.

Lara dodged away and drew her own knife, watching as Alex tried to step in front of her. She held up the knife so Powell and Alex could see it. "No!"

"You've got to be *kidding*," Alex said.

"You've got to be *going*," Lara told him.

"Lara! This is *insane!*" Alex waved his pistol. "Let me shoot him! *C'mon!*"

Lara had other plans and relieved Alex of his pistol. Still looking only at Powell, she gave Alex his marching orders.

"Leave *right now*," she commanded. "Get the others out of here safely. I'll follow."

Alex wiped perspiration from his forehead. "But—"

"*Right. Now. Go.*" Lara made her voice hard.

Reluctantly, but knowing he wasn't going to change her mind, Alex nodded. "I'll leave you a sled. Hurry." He nodded toward Powell. "Kick his butt."

Lara listened to Alex's retreating footsteps as she circled on Powell.

The cavern shuddered again, and for an instant Lara thought from the sound of it the whole place was going to collapse.

Powell pocketed one of his knives then drew his pistol.

Lara drew one of her pistols at the same time.

Powell grinned, then laid his pistol on the ground.

Lara placed her pistols on the ground as well.

"Lady Croft," Powell said smoothly as he held both knives again, waving them skillfully. "As we have only a few spare minutes before we both die, I suggest we use our time creatively." Without warning, he lunged at Lara.

Lara blocked the bared steel with her own blade, then blocked Powell's second attack with her forearm. From her own experience with knife-fighting, Lara knew such fights generally ended quickly. She parried Powell's strikes, then returned blinding ripostes. The screech of steel grinding against steel cut through even the thunder of the impending cavern collapse.

Powell was good. Lara knew that as she fought him. And she knew it would only be a matter of who made the first mistake. She was winded and covered with perspiration when Powell left an opening. Without hesitation, she took it, cutting him deeply, then knocking the stilettos from his hands.

Powell crumbled to the floor.

Bending down, breathing deeply, Lara took her father's pocket watch from Powell. "This belongs to me," she said.

"Take it," Powell gasped. "It runs a little fast anyway."

Still angry, Lara grabbed one of Powell's legs and dragged him across the floor like a sack of potatoes. She headed straight for the whirling timestorm. With the last bits of strength she had left, she hurled Powell into the timestorm.

Powell screamed as the raging time anomaly sucked him up into it.

Lara flicked open the pocket watch. "Ooops. Time to go."

Trapped and painfully tortured by the timestorm, Powell screamed at Lara as she walked away. *"Why won't you kill me!* I'm as good as dead."

Lara stopped briefly and glanced at the man that had killed her father. "Dead's not good enough."

"*Kill me!*" Powell shouted.

Lara started walking away and kept going. She spoke softly. "Good luck. As I said, you're going to need it."

She found the sled and dogs where Alex left them, sprinting the last few feet as one of the nearby cavern walls gave way in a rush of rumbling rock. The dogs pulled at their traces fretfully, more than ready to be off.

Lara stepped onto the sled, shook out the reins, and urged the dogs into a run. The sled's runners raced across the frozen cavern floor, pulling her toward the tomb's exit. She gazed up at the exit, watching as the eclipse continued passing. The sky lightened as the dogs ran upward.

"*Laaraaa!*" Powell screeched behind her.

The voice stayed with Lara as the dogs pulled the sled through the exit. Then the tomb collapsed completely behind her, shutting off the scream with a final, devastating *crunch*.

It was over.

EPILOGUE

Croft Manor, England

Lara climbed the Grand Staircase carefully. Arriving in her room, she looked at the bed with genuine regret. Before she could sleep, there was something else she knew she had to do.

She opened the closet and found only the floral-print dress still hanging there. She let out a long breath, then reached for the dress.

A few minutes later, Lara descended the staircase again, catching Hillary on his way up with a silver tea service.

When he looked up and saw Lara in the dress, he dropped the tea service in complete shock. "Oh my God!"

Lara ignored his reaction and she put on the straw hat she carried to complete the ensemble. She walked through the doors at the back of the house and into the garden to her father's memorial.

She took off the straw hat and stood wordlessly for a time, knowing that somewhere her father was there for her.

A bright yellow butterfly flew over the marble field tent, then winged into a tight spiral above it. A moment later, the butterfly shot off in another direction. Lara smiled as the beautiful insect flew high into the perfect blue sky.

Lara re-entered the house and stopped in her tracks.

A light strobed the room.

Hillary and Bryce stood at the top of the stairs. Another flash of light. Bryce held a Polaroid camera, the image of Lara in the dress developing from its mouth.

"For the history books," Hillary smiled.

Then in an instant life returned to normal for Lara Croft. The fully repaired droid wheeled from the equipment room. The drill fists had been replaced with cannon during Lara's absence.

A smile dawned on Lara's face as she regarded her opponent. She whipped the straw hat from her head, ready for action. After all, that was what she was born to do.

THE END

ABOUT THE AUTHOR

Mel Odom lives in Moore, Oklahoma, with his wife and five children. An avid gamer on the PlayStation 1 and 2, the Dreamcast, N64, and PC, Mel also writes strategy guides for games.

Besides the novelization for *Tomb Raider,* Mel has written novels for *Buffy the Vampire Slayer, Angel,* and *Sabrina the Teenage Witch.*